AN UNEXPECTED KISS

Half an hour later, Secundus walked around the outside of the house to the room where Helen had set up her office. He knocked softly on the French doors. No answer. Sec knocked again.

The door opened and Helen stood scowling in the doorway, squinting out at him. "Yes?"

"Yes? Just yes? Well, since you agree . . ." Sec put his hand at her waist, gently moving her inside as he followed. Almost before Helen knew for whom she'd reluctantly opened the door, he had bent to her, was kissing her. Awkwardly, her arms came up around his neck, and the kiss deepened. When he lifted his head, she lay her cheek against his chest, and for a long moment they stood silently. Sec sighed. "I shouldn't have done that." But his arms tightened around her.

"No. I shouldn't have responded." But she didn't move.

"Helen?"

"Yes, Sec?"

"I really shouldn't have."

"No."

"Because now, having had one, I don't think I can do without another. . . ."

BOOKS BY JEANNE SAVERY

Published by Zebra Books

Prologue

Two more days.

Secundus Alcester stared across the water from their anchorage in Plymouth Harbor. His ship had already been in quarantine for half the period required by law, but only now had Secundus left his cabin, the calm waters of the bay finally curing him of his easily roused *mal de mer*. He was beginning to believe he'd actually survived the voyage from India. The worst was over, yes, but he'd not yet achieved his goal. Secundus wished to continue. Immediately. But it wasn't to be.

Two more days!

Paulo da Silva, a Goan, stood patiently beside Secundus. He cast a considering eye over his friend. Secundus was not a good seaman. It had been an uncomfortable voyage. But Secundus was never one to pamper himself. "You are biting at the bit, are you not, my honored friend?"

"Chomping at the bit," corrected Secundus. He continued in a growl. "They let harlots aboard and then make them stay. Also those customs officials. Ridiculous. If there is sickness, they should allow no one *on* and if there is not, why may we not get off?"

"Whole cities have been ravaged by illness brought by unquarantined voyagers, honored son of most honorable Alcester."

Secundus nodded. "You do right to remind me." His scowl smoothed out and he chuckled. "It is only," he said much more pacifically, "that if I never feel another wave I shall have died happy." He stared again toward shore and experienced an unexpected and unsettling emotion. "Look, Paulo," he said softly. "It is England."

Obediently the Goan looked at the astonishing green of the fields. He felt no elation, no surge of happiness, no sense of homecoming. Paulo had left that behind. It was likely he'd never again see his homeland. But it was by his choice and he'd not regret it. "I am told one may hire carriage and horses to continue our journey, favored son."

"Hmmm? Travel post?" Secundus rubbed his nose. "I have it in my mind to experience the mail, Paulo. If the tales told are even half true . . . well!" After a moment he added, "I suppose one must reserve seats. Will you see to it?"

Paulo returned somewhat later laboring under a heavy load of disbelief.

"What is the matter, Paulo?"

"It is arranged." Paulo folded his hands and stared over Sec's shoulder at nothing in particular. "Inside seats are reserved for two on the Royal Mail coach."

"Spit it out, Paulo. What is it that bothers you?"

The Goan lost an internal argument concerning what is and what is not polite. "It is impossible," he blurted.

"*What* is impossible?"

"Someone is pre-var-i-cating." He drew out the recently learned word with care. "It must be that they prevaricate. I am told we board this coach at 9:39 one morning and arrive in London at 7:05 the next morning."

"So?"

"But I am also told this covers near three hundred English miles."

"That's about right, I think."

"But the speed with which one must travel, then. Fifteen miles per hour! It is impossible, surely."

"I am told the mails are the fastest things on the road, Paulo. Which is why I wish to try one."

Paulo studied his friend and mentor. The sea voyage had sapped Alcester's incredible strength. Perhaps it had affected his mind? Was he well enough to experience a journey so frightening? "I do not think I can bear it. Such speed." Paulo watched his friend with interest. Would he believe? Paulo sighed when Secundus grinned at him. So. He did not believe.

Secundus's uproarious laugh drew the eyes of the women who'd boarded to relieve the sailors of as much of their pay as might be managed. They'd turned a practiced eye on Sec when he'd appeared that morning, but with no luck. "Don't baby me, Paulo. I'm well enough," said Sec when he'd wiped away the tears with a final chuckle. "I'm my old self again—or soon will be."

Paulo fingered his rosary. He would try one more subterfuge. "It is my opinion that that which is called a post chaise is much more comfortable."

"You're doing it up much too brown, Paulo. Speed may be important and I'm no invalid." Secundus stared at the land he'd not seen for fifteen years. "Fifteen years," he murmured. Alcester's inner eye pictured an excessively shy young woman of astonishing intellect, a woman more plump than stylish, with an endearing stammer which disappeared as soon as one teased her into discussing things of interest to her. He recalled his first sight of her, of thinking she was little older than the village children gathered at her skirts, listening wide-eyed to her tales. He'd listened, too, and once she'd shooed the young ones off, he'd made himself known to her. It had taken patience to draw her out, to know her.

But, knowing her, it took no time at all to fall in love with her. He wondered where she was now.

Where his love might be was not relevant, of course, considering she was wed to another. He wondered if the marriage arranged by her father had been a terribly unhappy one. Most likely it had become like so many others once the heir was born: one went one's own way and ignored the other. But that, too, was not of immediate importance since there was nothing he could do.

What *was* important was finding and helping his niece and nephew who had been orphaned and left destitute— or the next thing to it—very nearly two years ago now. Two years. He and Paulo had been near Benares when the partially legible letter from his brother's solicitor finally caught up with them. What had become of his young relatives? What deprivations were they suffering? Sec pounded the rail with his fisted hand, again chomping at that bit to which Paulo had referred.

Two more days of this benighted quarantine before he could get on with it!

One

Almost exactly twenty-four hours after boarding the Falmouth-to-London Royal Mail in Plymouth, Secundus Alcester lowered his aching body from a musty smelling hackney. He'd hired the vehicle to bring him to Middle Temple Row from the Swan with Two Necks coaching establishment in Lad Lane where he'd been set down nearly two hours late. Putting his hands to the small of his back, he stared at the discreet brass plate inset beside the austere doorway to the family solicitor's office.

When the man's badly damaged letter, water stained and torn, had caught up with him, it had been clear on only two points: his brother was dead and his brother's family was suffering. Secundus had returned home by the fastest possible means, which included horses, a mean-spirited camel for too long a stage, and a trek into Goa. There he'd connected with a ship which carried him to Portugal where he'd caught another headed to England. Much of the journey had been uncomfortable—the camel and sea journey would ever be horrific memories. But the worst was over.

Unless unfinished business forced him to return to India. That notion was surprisingly distressing. Staring at the green fields surrounding Plymouth while waiting out quarantine and again while traveling up to London, Secundus had discovered he'd missed England. He didn't want to go away from it ever again. Late in the spring of the year the century was new, he had reluctantly taken a long last look at an English shore. He'd stayed abroad for fifteen years for a very good reason— or so he'd thought when young and, very likely, foolish. Now, home again, he was very nearly certain of it. That he'd been foolish, that is.

Secundus stretched, the cracking of his spine relieving some of the ache. "Well, Paulo," said Alcester, "we've arrived."

"So we have, honorable second son of most honored Alcester."

Sec turned a wry look on his traveling companion, the youngest son of an old and respected Goan family.

"Shall I apply the brass knocker to the wood of the door, son of . . . ?

"What you shall do," interrupted Sec, a trifle testily, "you miserable whelp of a dog-faced woman of the lowest caste of miserable wood cutters, is find yourself on the next ship east if you don't stop that play-acting." His eyes twinkled, belying the reprimand.

Paulo da Silva grinned, white teeth flashing in a face dark skinned by English standards. "Well? Shall I apply the brass to the wood?"

"Please do. Paulo?"

"Yes, my friend?" Paulo fingered his rosary. "Your desire?"

"Those formal phrases you love so much sit oddly on the English ear. If you don't cease using them you'll embarrass me."

"I would never wish to embarrass you."

"I know. That's why I gave you the hint."

Half an hour later Secundus wrapped up his interview with the solicitor. "Hmmm. To sum up, they were left with a pitiful remnant of the estate, still have a roof over their heads, and are not quite in the basket. I see. Now, was there anything else?" Sec rubbed his nose, wishing to ask about the woman he'd loved and left behind—a woman who had promised to wait for him, although her father had already promised her to another. He daren't make free with her name, but what of his oldest friend? "I don't suppose," he asked, "you'd know where Gubby Falconer might be found?" Almost before he'd finished speaking, Secundus shook his head. "No. Don't suppose you do. Seem to remember he's a member of White's. I'll inquire there."

The solicitor had almost ceased gobbling. "Gubb . . . *Gubby* . . . sir! Surely you couldn't . . . no, no, impossible." Secundus quirked an inquiring eyebrow. "You can't be referring to Sir Augustus Falconer?"

"Sir Augustus, you say?" Secundus grinned. "By Ol' Nick's nightcap, Gubby's a baronet, is he? Last I knew he had no expectations. Must have been four or five lives in the way of his advancement. Well, well. Sir Gubby! I'll tease him about that, I will." He chuckled all the way down the dirty stairs and out into the street.

"Now let me think," said Secundus. "That way we hit the Fleet at about Temple Bar. It becomes the Strand, which we follow to Pall Mall, and at its end we'll catch St. James's where we'll find White's. I hope Gubby's in town," he added. "I can trust his eye when picking me a pair and the black I want for young Robert. Late to make good on old promises, I suppose, but at least I didn't forget. Then I'll drop by a tailor's before we drive down to Lewes—Gubby will recommend me to the best. And boots—I need boots. And hats." He sighed. "Since my relatives aren't languishing in a workhouse, we'll take a day or two extra and see to such things, but we won't dawdle." He frowned. "Who'd have thought my brother would develop gambling fever."

"You will forebear to see, at once, if your lady has faithfully awaited your return?" Sec's normally jovial features hardened, his eyes glinting as they did when angry or upset. Paulo decided he was upset. "I will place a small wager with you, oh second son. I wager she has faithfully awaited your return." The Goan fingered the new ivory crucifix blessed by an uncle, his family's priest. He hid all but the merest hint of a smile.

"There isn't a chance of it. Her father was a cold man, Paulo, and she a great tease. Sometimes, when I've felt my lowest, I've wondered if she favored me—such an unworthy suitor—to force his attention. At the last her brother informed me a marriage had been arranged. Most likely she's an established matron, fat as a flawn, and half a dozen brats to her credit. And very likely," he added thoughtfully, "unwilling to give me the time of day."

"What is a flawn, honored sir?"

"A word you don't know? A flawn, my erudite friend, is an exceedingly rich and heavy pancake."

Paulo nodded. "Even so, I think you impatient to find your lady."

Secundus sighed. "I am, Paulo. I am. Wish it weren't necessary to look into my kin's affairs, but then," he said, brightening, "one wouldn't wish to visit one's female friends before one's tailor finished with one, would one?"

"Peacock," teased Paulo slyly, sliding his gaze sideways.

"Hmmm." Secundus's eyes twinkled in response. "The *Alice May* was supposed to be in port about now, if I remember rightly. I wonder if you'd be happiest returning to Goa when she goes."

"If she kept to schedule," responded Paulo promptly. "She weighed anchor with the tide the twenty-fifth. That would be day before yesterday."

"Then, since she's very likely gone," said Secundus morosely, "I suppose I must put up with your impertinence yet awhile. It is too bad."

The two men, at ease with each other as only old friends can be, chuckled. But, when Alcester stopped before White's and the door opened, Paulo assumed the role of perfect secretary, one he adopted when he willed, whether Secundus thought it necessary or not. Alcester had given up trying to change Paulo. He had wished to give the Goan a place in his business—as he had some of the da Silva family, one uncle heading the Bombay office and a brother captaining one of Sec's ships—but, from the moment Secundus saved Paulo's life from a rampaging bull elephant, Paulo had devoted himself to serving Sec's interests in more menial ways and continued to refuse the offer.

So Secundus put up with Paulo's quirks, called him friend, and trusted him with business and personal secrets. Sec needed him and was very glad Paulo had come with him to England, but he didn't understand the why of it. Paulo would hate the food and suffer from the colder climate.

"Sir Augustus Falconer?" The porter looked Alcester's travel-worn figure up and down and tilted his nose a trifle higher. "Your card, please." He extended a salver.

Sec put on a wide-eyed look of innocence and patted his pockets. "Damme if I have one on me. Just take ol' Gubby a message, will you?" He slipped a coin in the man's ready hand. "Tell him this riddle: Second in love. Second in war. Winner always. Who is it?" The porter trotted off, leaving them kicking their heels in the hall.

"Second in love?" a voice roared from an interior room. "Out of my way, man. Move! I thought the bastard dead these ten years and more. Where is he? Secundus, old man," said Sir Augustus, his arms wide, his face one huge grin. The two greeted each other enthusiastically before the baronet pushed his taller and much slimmer friend back so he could look at him. "Brown as a well-seasoned piece of walnut. What *have* you been doing with yourself?" Taking Sec's arm, he drew him along the hall, sticking his balding head through one doorway after another until he found a room which was empty. "Well, now," grinned Sir Augustus Falconer, patting his well-rounded tummy. "Well, now."

Secundus grinned, too. He hadn't returned to England and immediately found his lost love, but it was very nearly as soul satisfying to see, again, this friend of his youth.

That same evening, in a big old manor house near a village not far from Lewes on the north side of the South Downs in Sussex, Alcester's niece, Ruth Alcester, tucked the covers more firmly around Tibby and stared fondly at her curly-headed little half sister. Fairies in the woods, indeed. Was it wrong to indulge the children in the fairy tales they loved? Surely it was innocent pleasure. But she must remember to caution Tibby the stories were merely stories and such things didn't really happen. "Go to sleep, Tibby. It's late, child."

Ruth returned to the kitchen where Robert sat with a London newspaper. The vicar had passed it to Robert, having had it from the squire, who had bought it when last he rode into Lewes. When they finished with it, Ruth would take it to Miss Brown, the retired governess who lived beyond the village.

"Peter and Marie are asleep, but Tibby is restless." Ruth eyed her brother, who, only ten months younger, was often mistaken for her twin. He folded the paper and laid it aside with a yawn. "Robert," she asked, "if we hadn't agreed you'd take responsibility for the children, what would you have done when Father died?"

"When he topped his worst folly by the ultimate in cowardly behavior and shot himself, you mean?"

Ruth bit her lip, looking, for a moment, very like eight-year-old Tibby. "I hadn't realized you were so bitter."

"Not with you. And certainly not with the little ones. But it all seems so hopeless, sometimes." Robert met her eyes. "Mr. Chalmers came by today." When Ruth would have interrupted, Robert said, "I know he is forever predicting doom and gloom, but I fear he's talking sense this time. If our tenants find themselves in difficulty . . ." Ruth grimaced and Robert nodded. "Exactly. Chalmers made his usual offer for our land, then warned me that if things get bad, his next would be lower." Robert stared into the empty grate. "I've been thinking it might not be a bad idea." He didn't see the stricken look crossing Ruth's face. "After buying Peter's place on a ship, we'd still have enough money . . ." He looked up. "We could emigrate, Ruth. To Pennsylvania—or even Kentucky—a new start for us."

Ruth's hands clenched around Peter's shirt, which needed mending. Was Robert serious? "Why give Peter so much?"

"Peter has only one ambition, and he'll be good for nothing else. I hate to think what may happen to the boy if he isn't helped to a ship." Robert sighed. "Perhaps I should write his mother's cousin again. I don't understand why the old gentleman hasn't retrieved his promise to Peter."

"It was very nice of him to send the children guineas last Christmas," said Ruth. Little Tibby had told Ruth to save hers, "for 'mergencies, like if Peter broke his other arm and the doctor grumbled about coming to a house which never paid its bills." It wasn't right a child should be so cognizant of their problems that she'd give up her Christmas gift. And wasn't her newest game a sign of the same unchildish concern for her family?

"Why are you frowning, Ruth?"

"Tibby. She has the grandest imagination, Rob."

"She does indeed. What is it this time?"

"Fairies in the woods. She happened to notice them, she said, when looking for a stray leprechaun. She wished to make him give her his gold so we'd be rich again and not have to worry so much, you see."

"What an amazing infant it is."

Rob's chuckle drew a quickly fading smile from Ruth. "She shouldn't have to have such silly daydreams. Sometimes I actually dislike our father. It wasn't right to throw away his fortune."

"At least he had the courtesy to take himself out of it before he lost every last bit," said her brother dryly.

"I sometimes wonder if that was a kindness. We've just enough that we manage, with great difficulty, to hang on to our precious gentility."

"Which is why I wonder if we ought to emigrate. In Pennsylvania one may buy a great deal of land very cheaply," he said quietly. "I've heard an acre costs as little as a laborer's day wage here. Think what we could do with the sale of this property!"

Ruth didn't want to think about it, about moving. Again. Before their father bought the Morris property, he'd moved them hither and yon, until their mother died. Then he'd put them into schools, which changed with his fortunes. Upon retiring, he'd bought the manor and brought them home. At last. It hadn't bothered Ruth when he'd rewed. In fact, she'd been of an age to need a woman's advice and understanding. It had been a shock when the second Mrs. Alcester died. Not only had Ruth lost a friend but their father became a stranger to them as well. Ruth would do nearly anything rather than move again.

A vision of petite, golden-haired Lucinda Chalmers entered her mind. Was her desire to remain in the only home she'd every known quite fair to Robert, who must continue to see the love he'd never have? Besides, wasn't there another, selfish, reason she wished to stay? Ruth compressed her lips and bent over her work. While they lived here, she'd glimpse Lord Rotherford now and again, see the sun gleaming off ash blond hair above dark-lashed eyes and brows, observe the wide shoulders . . . her heart beat faster, her blood heating with the thought . . . If they moved, she'd never see him again. The heat turned to a sickness in the pit of her stomach. It churned. Everything in her rejected the notion of never again seeing Rotherford.

"Robert," she asked abruptly, "is it something we must decide at once, this notion of emigrating?"

"I've thought for months now, and can't decide. That's why I mentioned it. Perhaps, together, we can make the right decision for all of us."

"If only Uncle Secundus hadn't dropped off the face of the earth."

Robert looked up. "Lord, I haven't thought of him in years." He chuckled. "I was Tibby's age, wasn't I, when he left? He promised me a pony, black I think, when he'd made his fortune, remember?"

"Hmmm. I thought it a silly sort of gift. I was coveting something much more sensible—a new blue dress if I remember correctly."

Ruth and Robert traded other stories of their long-lost uncle. Their eyes met, held. It was dear memories such as these that made them a family, thought Ruth.

The wish for their uncle's homecoming was, Ruth knew, much akin to little Tibby's uncaught leprechaun.

Uncle Secundus was just as likely to appear! At their father's death, his solicitor promised an attempt would be made to find their uncle. Nothing had come of it. Ruth smiled at the notion of an envelope sealed into oiled cloth, moving around the globe, following faint traces of a wanderer, who, if not dead, must surely be more destitute than they were themselves. Because it he weren't, they'd have heard from him long ago. Wouldn't they?

She decided she had nearly as much imagination as little Tibby because, although she couldn't believe in the existence of fairies, she *could* believe that Uncle Secundus, if he were here, would somehow solve their problems. Mr. Chalmers would find Robert an acceptable match for Lucy, and their uncle would get Peter the ship the boy wanted so badly.

Oh yes. She could dream just as well as Tibby when she put her mind to it. She could even dream she might somehow become an acceptable bride for a peer who, for reasons she didn't understand, no longer knew she was alive. She could see herself dressed in her favorite blue made up in the latest style; miraculously, she'd have learned to dance that daring new dance, the waltz—and of course her partner for the dance would be none other than Lord Rotherford himself.

Ruth cast a guilty glance at her brother. He was leaning back in his chair, something very close to a snore issuing from his slightly open mouth. Poor Rob. He worked so hard. She should wake him and send him to bed . . . and she would. Very soon. Just as soon as she'd finished that waltz with her dream love. Ruth, too, put her head back and closed her eyes.

The first of August was not only the anniversary of the ascension of the House of Hanover to the throne of England, but also, and more important to such a little girl, it was Marie Alcester's eighth birthday. To celebrate it, the Alcesters took a picnic out onto the downs. Once it was finished, everyone but motherly little Tibby, who knew exactly how far she was allowed to wander, went home. Tibby lay back against a boulder and munched a last custard tart as she mulled over her family's problems. Life could be very difficult, thought the little girl. If only there were something one could do.

But Ruth said holidays were rare and not to be wasted. Tibby, an obedient child, quite happily invented an imaginary game to play all by herself which, eventually, brought her near the fish pond on the edge of Lord Rotherford's estate. A stray glance across the water brought Tibby up short, blinking, her game abruptly forgotten. Could it be? Surely not. She couldn't believe it. Going closer, Tibby spread the reeds and improved her view. Impossible. But it was just like in the book: a bare chest where a shirt gaped open and the exceedingly full trousers.

Oh dear. *Peter wouldn't be afraid just because they'd found a genie.* Tibby was fearful right down to her dirty jean half-boots. But she was also determined. Ruth too often worried where to find their next guinea when they hadn't so much as a sixpence. Robert spent every hour in the garden, or fixing something, and he, too, often worried about sixpences. Peter should take up his life at sea. And Marie? Could anything be done for sweet little Marie?

Oh, dear. It was time to stop thinking and time to do—as Ruth so often said—even if one did tremble all over. Approaching one hesitant step at a time, Tibby stared at the genie's puffy-bottomed trousers, which were caught at the ankles with pretty pearl buttons. She admired the bright red sash, too . . . but shouldn't the

creature wear heelless slippers with pointy toes instead
of low boots with tiny spurs attached? Tibby shrugged.
The important thing was to catch him before he disappeared and, still more important, that he not cheat her
out of her wishes. She tiptoed closer, only to jump back
with a squeak when the creature woke, sat up, and
looked around. Tibby's genie smiled sleepily.

"What have we here?" he asked. Lieutenant Gerald
Ralston groped behind him, found and shook out the
coat he'd used as a pillow, and, putting it on, buttoned
some of its buttons. "Hello, little maid," he said. Tibby
pounced, grasping the genie's sleeve. Her eyes widened
and she bit her lip. "Now, what's this, child? Don't you
go puffing creases in my new jacket." The genie tugged
gently at her fingers.

"Can't let go." Tibby caught a better grip. The lieutenant, lately of the Rifles, politely asked the determined
child to explain herself. "Can't let go 'til you give me my
wishes."

"Wishes?" Gerry blinked. His mind, he decided, must
still be fogged with sleep. Or perhaps he was still dreaming? "I don't understand."

She made a sound of exasperation before warning
him, "I know what you are, so don't try to fool me."

"What am I, then?"

"A genie, o'course." Tibby tossed her curls, a scornful
note coloring her young voice. "I caught you fair, so you
must give me three wishes like in the story and no tricks,
mind," she added sternly, staring at him with that
solemn unvarying stare of the young.

The lieutenant, ignoring the rest, asked, "I'm a what?"

"A genie. From a bottle. Or maybe the other kind?"
Tibby frowned. "A lamp genie? Ruth 'plained there were
two sorts."

Gerry scowled at his Petersham trousers. He'd had a

foreboding the new design was a mistake and just see what had happened! "What if I said I'm not a genie at all? Or maybe only a sort of genie . . . an apprentice genie," he added, quickly, when the child's eyes glistened with unshed tears.

Tibby blinked back all but one glittery teardrop. "Do you still give three wishes?" she asked, worried.

The lieutenant found he was amused by the big-eyed, golden-haired, and, at the moment, dirty child. Visions of dolls and sweets danced in his head. Instead of telling her to take herself off, as he very likely ought to do, he suggested, "You tell me your wishes and I'll think about it." Tibby bit her lip. "If I promise not to escape, will you let go my sleeve?" he asked.

"I don't want to be tricked."

"I promise I won't trick you." Visions of ponies or lace-trimmed dresses followed the sweetmeats through Gerry's imagination. "But I can't promise to fill your wishes either. Apprentice genies aren't very good at it yet, or they wouldn't be apprentices, would they?"

Tibby decided to trust him—partly—and reached for his sash. "I'm afraid to let you go entirely," she explained. "It's important, you see, that I get my wishes. Now please be quiet while I think."

Obligingly, Lieutenant Ralston leaned back on his elbows. His waif was about ten, he thought, misled by the odd maturity of the eight-year-old as well as the Alcester tendency to a tall stature. She was too well spoken to be, as he'd first assumed, a village child, so who might she be? Squire Chalmers? No. Too young. Vicar wasn't married. Gerry remembered a retired naval man had moved into the neighborhood, but the man was dead, wasn't he? There'd been a scandal . . . A slight tug at his sash distracted him. How serious the child was. He felt an urge to tell her to stop biting her lip, that she was too young to worry so. Besides, how difficult could it be to decide between a big box of sweets and a doll?

"I've decided on my first wish."

"Have you? Remember, I'm only an apprentice and can't snap my fingers to fill your wish. It'll take time, assuming I can fill it at all, of course."

"I remember Ruth and Robert talking. . . ."

"Who are they?"

His imp looked as if he were a very stupid genie not to know something so important, but replied politely enough. "My brother and sister." Her genie seemed to require more, so she said, "They worry. Especially Ruth."

"And why do they worry?"

"Don't you know anything?"

"Remember I'm only an apprentice genie. You must help me all you can."

"Oh," she said, accepting that. "Because they're responsible now." When her genie frowned, she continued in a careful, kind, explaining way. "They are our guardians. So we can all stay together, o'course, so there'll be laughter and happy times, all of us together."

Light dawns, thought Gerry. The naval man had bought the Morris manor and then—Gerald remembered the bit of forgotten gossip—he'd gambled most of it away before putting a period to his existence. No wonder Robert and Ruth worried. He wondered that the family could laugh at all. It seemed a long time since *he'd* last laughed. Gerald pushed that thought aside. "Was your father a sea captain?" The smile that lit the child's face was worth a few wrinkles in his coat, decided Gerald. In fact, it was worth a lot of wrinkles. He quirked an eyebrow. "Well?"

She nodded. "You are doing very well for a 'prentice, aren't you? There's just five of us now. Marie is six and I'm eight and a half and Peter's twelve and Robert's old and Ruth's a year older than that. But that's not important." Tibby bit her lip hard, the permanent little line between her brows deepening. "My wish. It's so hard to be sure I don't waste it, but I *think* I should ask for coal. Ruth and Robert wondered what they might sell to buy it before it gets so 'spensive like it does when winter comes and everyone needs it." An odd maturity settled on the very young shoulders as she quoted from the overheard conversation.

"That," he said, "makes a great deal of good sense."

"The coal?" she asked, the earnest look very much in place.

"I'll think of a way to manage coal," he responded solemnly.

"I wish I could be sure. . . ." The child's head bent, that lip tucked between her small white teeth.

When the pause lengthened, Gerry, tongue in cheek, suggested, "Maybe you need another man around. A husband for your Ruth, perhaps?"

Tibby considered. "But what if you picked the wrong one?"

"Do you think she has her eye on a particular man?" Tibby nodded that solemn wide-eyed nod. "Just who is he?" Tibby looked at him, her head to one side. "I can't help if I don't know," he added. Gerald firmly squelched the little voice which told him prying into a lady's secrets was an exceedingly ungentlemanly thing to do. But somehow this whole interlude wasn't quite real, so it didn't matter, did it? That thought brought him up short. It *was* real. This was *not* a dream. His imp expected her wishes to be filled. My Lord, he thought, aghast, what have I gotten myself into?

"You could help if you knew his name?"

"No! Definitely not. Apprentice genies can't possibly help with such hard wishes. Much too difficult except for the very most experienced sort of genie." A muscle jerked in Gerry's jaw. "I think you better ask for something simple and be done with it."

The perpetual frown line between Tibby's eyes creased deeply. Then, "Oh, of course!" She smiled that brilliant smile. "What you said about a man. It needn't be a husband for Ruth, need it?"

"I don't suppose it need be," said Gerry cautiously, wondering what his imp had up her overly tight sleeve now.

"I was listening to Robert and Ruth last night." She gave him a mischievous look. "Ruth says I shouldn't do that. That it isn't right to . . . to . . . what's the word?"

Gerry's brows clashed. "Eavesdrop?"

She nodded, obviously unconcerned with the ethics of her behavior. "But I did and I know exactly what to wish. You find my Uncle Se-cun-dus Alcester, please," she enunciated carefully. "I didn't know we *had* an uncle isn't that strange? He went away to make his fortune so he can get Peter a ship and Ruth a husband. Why"—her eyes grew large—"if you make that wish come true, then you don't need to worry about the coal, do you?"

Gerry, understanding what the child wanted, winced. He'd gotten himself into deep water this time. "That's a very hard wish for an apprentice genie," he said cautiously. "Even for a real genie it would be difficult. Think, child. To find one person in all this great world? How would one even begin?"

"I understand." She nodded solemnly. "You are only a 'prentice, so it's very hard for you."

"What a wise little girl you are." Her sad face was more than he could bear. "Come child, cheer up, now. Think up something else. Something easy. If you forget about your uncle, then you've two wishes still in hand," he added slyly.

An equally sly look settled on Tibby's features. "I don't have to ask all my wishes at once," she reminded him. She tipped her head to a stubborn angle. "And maybe I'm wasting my wish, but you've warned me, so that's fair, but it would be the very best thing if Uncle Se-cun-dus came home, so, even if it's hard, please try."

"Child, I don't want to disappoint you."

"That's nice," said Tibby, her face lighting up and her hand coming out to grasp his. She dropped it immediately and looked at her dirty palm, glancing up at him with a guilty expression.

Gerry smiled. He liked this odd child, but he wondered if he were dicked in the nob and not because he fell asleep at the drop of an eyelid, anywhere and at anytime, and *had* done ever since Waterloo. For a moment he let the horror of that last battle wash over him, the death of so many friends. He focused on the wide-eyed angel, patiently waiting. *Was* he ready for Bedlam? He must be, because he'd decided to try to find the lost uncle. "I'll try, child, but I doubt my success. When did he go?"

"When Robert was my age," she said promptly, then added, wonderingly. "That was before I was borned, I think."

Before his imp was borned? Ten—no, eight and a half years? And just how many years ago was this Robert, who was old but a year younger than Ruth, a mere eight and a half! "So very long ago? Angel, this will take some thinking. And," he said, casting a knowledgeable eye toward the sun's position, "it's time for me to be getting home."

The line deepened between the child's brows. "You'll not forget you owe me one more wish, will you? And you'll think about the coal since you might not find my uncle?"

Gerry suppressed an impulse to rub the frown from the child's brow. "I'll not forget. I promise. Be off with you, now, my little one. You can find me here most afternoons." Gerry watched his obedient imp run off and shook his head at his own foolishness. The coal was bad enough, but finding a man who had disappeared years ago? He grinned ruefully. Dear ol' Uncle Hubee—John, that was—would have him clapped up in Bedlam for even thinking of trying to find the man!

How *did* one search the world for a long-lost uncle?

Two

So, about the time Secundus and Sir Augustus—having been to the bootmaker and a supplier of fine linen—were thinking seriously of discussing a fine beefsteak in the dining room at White's, Gerry turned over ways of finding the long-lost—and very likely dead—man. He'd ask his uncle, of course, although John would very likely think him mad. But Helen wouldn't. Now *that* might be the answer. His aunt, Helen Rotherford, was to arrive soon to plan the Rotherford's annual garden party and she'd do her possible to help him help the Alcesters. So, the coal was a certain bet . . . but the child was right—finding the uncle might well solve all the family's problems, and finding the man was a bigger problem than any he'd ever faced.

His aunt's letter, reluctantly agreeing to be hostess for yet another year, had arrived that morning. She'd protested taking on the duty—again. John, she'd written, was thirty-one years old. It was time he married, provided his own hostess, and stopped pestering her. At the ripe age of thirty-four she wished to retire from such nonsense, thank you just the same. She was far too busy, she wrote, to waste time on frivolity.

Gerry chuckled at the thought of Helen indulging in anything which might be defined as frivolous. She was very much the blue-stocking, kindhearted to a fault and with so much character people quickly forgot she had no beauty as the ton thought of beauty. Helen had a presence which derived from self-knowledge and self-confidence. Then, too, she had good bones so that with maturity and a thinning down of an overly plump young body, strong attractive features had been revealed which she'd likely carry to her grave.

Gerry put such thoughts aside as he entered the library, looking for John and a tankard or two of good home-brew. "Dear old Uncle Hubee, so *there* you are," he said with well-feigned insouciance.

"Give over, will you? The preferred name is John . . . as you well know." Lord Rotherford lounged before the empty grate, his long legs stretched out and neatly crossed at the ankles. He peered from under lowered lids in an attempt to determine his nephew's state of mind, but Gerald was too good at hiding how he felt. "More to the point, Gerry, how do *you* do?"

"The same." Gerald shrugged. "I sleep and sleep and wonder if I'll ever feel like a full day's hunting or like dancing all night . . . as I did not so very long ago. If there wasn't a grubby little handprint on the sleeve of my new coat, I'd wonder if I'd taken to dreaming wild dreams as well."

"Handprint?" Rotherford's heavy brows drew close over deep-set dark eyes which contrasted strangely with his ashy blond hair. "Some village child?"

"Not so. My imp is the orphaned daughter of your late neighbor to the west. Captain Alcester." Rotherford's finely delineated lips twisted in distaste. "Left numerous children and very little else, if I've guessed correctly," Gerald said, ending on a questioning note.

"The oldest boy was named guardian, I believe, there being no relatives found willing to take in the youngsters."

Gerald nodded. "That would be Robert."

"I see she held on long enough to get your sympathy. Was she begging? How much did she get from you?"

"Beg? My imp?" Gerry's outrage, although exaggerated, was real. "Nothing of the sort. She mistook me for a genie," he said. His brows arched into a rueful look. "You may now say I told you so, since you warned me against these trousers." John chuckled. "She'd caught me fair and square and, having caught me, she demanded three wishes—no tricking her, either. What's the oldest sister like?"

"Miss Alcester?" Rotherford's eyes went blank. Without moving a muscle, he gave the impression he'd withdrawn.

For a moment Gerry eyed the man who was more brother than uncle. He'd never seen quite *that* look on John's face. "According to my imp, her sister worries."

Rotherford's brows snapped together. Then his eyes met Gerry's curious gaze. "Dear me," he drawled, "does the child expect you to do something about that? Don't involve me in any plans you make. If you are *me*, m'boy, you must watch for the encroachment of all sorts of mushrooms . . . and the Alcesters, since the father's death, are become the worst sort of mushroom." Would Gerry buy such intolerance? Very likely not. Blast the woman. Why couldn't he put Ruth Alcester from his mind? Most recently he'd seen her holding the youngest, the two of them nose to nose, laughing, delightful. . . .

Gerry's voice interrupted John's thoughts. "It is my belief they are not the least bit encroaching. What's more, you don't believe it either."

Rotherford sighed. It had been a foolish impulse, the attempt to denigrate a family who didn't deserve his scorn.

"In fact, dear ol' unc, I do need help with my imp's wishes."

"To buy sugarplums and a doll? Come, Gerry, you can handle that sort of thing without my aid . . . and without being drawn in by the elder Alcesters." Rotherford ground his teeth. Surely he hadn't just tried the same stupid trick a second time.

"You don't understand, John. My problem is far more difficult than a bag of sweetmeats. Coal. One should get winter coal, now," he said, his tongue firmly in cheek, "while it's cheap, you know."

Rotherford blinked, a sleepy look settling over his features, which often fooled people into thinking he was disinterested, but it didn't deceive Gerry. "Coal?" Rotherford drank off his ale. "The child asked for coal?"

"A most interesting imp, dear uncle mine. A little golden-haired angel with dirty hands." A smile hovered around Gerry's mouth. "There was also a smear of mud on the tip of her nose." A chuckle, rather rusty, startled both men; they stared at each other. "She's sweet as a lamb, my minx, and more solemn than your spaniel bitch that time she had too many pups to run after."

Rotherford smiled at the memory. Gerry grinned back. Suddenly they lurched from their chairs and pounded each other on the back, laughter, free and golden, drifting around them. Healing laughter. Rotherford raised his eyes toward the ceiling, a thank you, Lord, in his heart. Maybe Gerald was truly getting better, would no longer drift around the house like a ghost, his eyes sad and his spirits low.

When they were again seated and holding full tankards, Rotherford raised his in a toast. "To your imp, Gerry."

"To my imp, but do put on your thinking cap," he coaxed.

Rotherford had forgotten the coal in his delight that Gerry had laughed. Enjoying Gerry's story of the encounter was one thing, but to become involved with the Alcesters? Not at all wise. His brows rose in query. "Explain to me why I should care to help my late improvident neighbor's children?"

"Because I liked my cherub very much indeed," said Gerald promptly. His expression softened. "She woke me up, John, made me want to stay awake." He bit his lip, his gaze shifting away, back, steadying. "John," he said, "for the first time since Waterloo something seems worth doing and that perhaps it's all right that I'm alive when so many died. Do you understand, John?"

Gerry's words silenced all Rotherford's objections. The lieutenant had arrived from the Continent soon after Waterloo, mazy and exhausted. His condition had had Rotherford in a fever of concern because nothing would penetrate Gerry's malaise—until now.

If the Alcesters' problems pulled his nephew out of the doldrums, then the acquaintance must be encouraged, despite his decision he must avoid Miss Alcester. When the family first moved into the manor, Ruth Alcester had been a long-legged, gangling filly of a girl, her future attractions not yet obvious. Whenever they met, Rotherford had treated her in a lightly teasing manner. But the girl had matured into a lovely statuesque woman. A woman with whom he allowed himself only one dance at the rare parties where they occasionally met, and a woman with whom he never flirted. Miss Ruth Alcester, impoverished gentry, was not someone with whom an honorable man toyed, no matter how much the notion appealed. Now, however, for Gerry's sake, he must overcome the fact that merely thinking of her aroused him to lustful thoughts. He sighed.

Misunderstanding the tenor of that sigh, Gerry said, "Helen will help me if you can't. Did she say she'd arrive Sunday or Monday? She didn't sound very happy about it, did she? Does she truly wish to retire from Society?"

Gerry's questions had the unfortunate result of reminding Rotherford of Helen's letter. His response was caustic. "My sister considers herself a spinster, but re-tire?" growled John. "She should spend more time with the people who can help her. *Retire!* Definitely not. The money to support her charities can be found only in So-ciety." Concern drew John's brows into a vee. "But, more important, she must abandon going among the mill workers and miners and into slums." John glared at Gerry as if it were his fault.

"Don't look to me," Gerry argued. "I've never known how to keep Helen from doing something she believes she should do, or, to the contrary, make her do something she thinks she shouldn't."

Rotherford grimaced. "That's the nut right out of the shell of the problem. There was only ever one man with the knack of making Helen see sense. Then he disappeared, never to be heard from again—not that it's likely I'd ap-prove of him for Helen now, any more than I did then."

"Oh? Who?"

"Secundus Alcester—uncle to your imp," said Rother-ford, a dry note roughening his voice.

Gerry looked toward the heavens and silently ques-tioned whether someone up there was having a bit of fun. So Secundus Alcester had once been a suitor of Helen's. How very interesting. "I don't suppose," he asked casually, "you'd know how to go about finding the man, would you?"

"Alcester? Why should I want to?"

"Because, my dear o' Hubee-Dubee, after the simple wish—relatively speaking—for coal, my precious imp's second wish is that I do just that—I'm to find her uncle, Secundus Alcester."

Whenever Miss Helen Rotherford returned to Rother Hall, she indulged herself by stopping at Lewes. It was, after all, only a small treat or perhaps just an exercise in nostalgia, a pilgrimage into the past? She panted slightly as she hurried up the steep, narrow street leading to the ruined castle and passed through the ancient gate. Above her hung the ancient portcullis, still threatening. She climbed on, this time up worn steps, onto the battlements, her thoughts on an age when men wearing chain mail patrolled the walls. The world was surely a better place since a time when no one was safe from his neighbor and every lord a petty tyrant.

Helen laid her hands on the crumbling parapet and looked out at the rolling, tree-covered countryside. A field of stubble reminded her of the proposed corn laws and she scowled. Modern landholders were very nearly as bad as those old despots, she thought. It was in their interest, after all, that corn laws be passed, laws protecting the high price of wheat. If passed, there'd be few imports of grain, no cheap bread, and many a hungry belly. On the other hand, the surgeon, Edward Jenner, had defeated smallpox. The mills produced yards and yards of cheap cloth, and the poor were better clothed then ever before. But the hunger. Oh dear, the hunger.

The sound of voices intruded. An East India man and his servant, she decided, peering around the edge of her hood, although the rosary the darker man toyed with indicated he was a Catholic rather than a Hindu.

Helen frowned. The tall Englishman reminded her of . . . but no. Nonsense. It couldn't be. Others, over the years, had reminded her of Secundus Alcester only, always, to prove to be strangers. Fearing she'd be accosted, Helen turned away before, accidentally, she met the eyes of either man. Such a reprehensible character you are, she scolded herself. She should have brought her maid with her—and would have if the silly woman didn't chatter so. She peered again. The two men, each with his hands clasped behind him, strolled on, deep in discussion. Relieved she'd not found herself in a difficult, if not dangerous, situation, Helen walked the other way along the wall to the nearest steps and speedily returned to her private parlor at the inn.

Then, knowing she had only a few minutes before dinner was served, Helen allowed herself to daydream of a man she hadn't seen for fifteen years. It was a vision of the two of them standing side by side up there on the ramparts where she'd just stood alone, a minor self-indulgence. Just a brief dream of what might have been, the *should* have been. A serving man, bearing a tray, knocked just then. Helen's maid opened the door for him. The dream was ended before barely begun. She put away thoughts more suitable to a young miss just out of the schoolroom and decided she'd order the horses put to once the meal was finished, and continue to the Hall. There was part of a moon and no distance, really, to go. It would be best. . . .

Paulo followed his friend up worn steps to the battlements overlooking Lewes. Secundus traced the mortar where unbeknownst to him Helen Rotherford had placed her hands not five minutes earlier. He picked at it, his eyes focused somewhere beyond the town. Always sensitive to moods, Paulo allowed their interesting discussion about Alcester's London office to drop. Finally Secundus sighed. Paulo's teeth showed briefly, then disappeared. That look. So revealing. "You came here with her?" Paulo asked politely.

Secundus swiped at his face as if ridding it of cobwebs. "Helen. Yes. We said goodbye. Right in this place I told her I was leaving and that I hadn't a notion if I'd ever come back. It was the last time I saw her. She'd returned to Rother Hall soon after her father refused my offer for her hand, and I'd come down to see my brother." Secundus's eyes came into focus and he stared at Paulo. "You did it again."

"Did it?"

"You got me talking about things I've sworn I'd never discuss. But I do want to talk, especially since I may see her soon—if I dare—once I've sorted out my family, that is." Sec pulled up memories he'd deliberately buried. "I was a second son, as you are all too aware—you tease me often enough. Our father wasn't very lucky, picking up prize money, and we grew up with all the elements to make us gentlemen except the single most important: wealth. In fact, it wasn't easy buying my brother's commission. I never grudged him it, however. I'm sure Primus made a demmed fine officer. Me?" Secundus grinned, a wry twist to his lips. "You know how it is with me in a heavy sea, Paulo."

"Most any sea," said Paulo. He shared Sec's mirth, although at the time it was anything but funny. Secundus Alcester had suffered a great deal. Paulo suspected dread of *mal de mer* had, perhaps, kept his friend in India far longer than it had taken him to amass a fortune—dread, and a true enjoyment of the machinations necessary to make money in that country.

"In any case, sailing wasn't for me. I drifted, not knowing what I wished to do. Eventually Primus bought his manor house and I met my Helen." Sec's eyes shifted back out of focus, and Paulo, ever patient, waited quietly for him to begin again. "She was . . . special, Paulo. She didn't flirt like other girls, but looked you square in the eye. She wasn't a beauty, my overly plump little robin. But she attracted attention because she . . . she . . . she drew eyes even though she wasn't one of the incomparables because she . . . I don't know . . . she had character, I guess. Anyway, I followed her back to London when the Season began that spring."

"So you loved her and wished to wed her."

"Since I loved her, I trotted around to her father and did the proper thing. He took a look at my pittance—I hadn't so much as a competence in those days. He asked, politely, about my prospects—which were, of course, nil—and he showed me the door." Sec dipped his head in a particularly Indian movement, denoting acceptance of the inevitable. "That evening I met Helen at another ton party. She knew of a little room where we could be quiet. I told her I must cease to think of her, that we must part. She suggested we elope."

Paulo's brows climbed his forehead. He had seen an unhappy British bride snubbed by other officers' wives merely because she'd eloped with her husband before his regiment was shipped to India. It had been, he thought, a very unpleasant situation. Sec's Helen had been willing to contravene that particular taboo of this strange country.

"We fought when I refused. She refused to take no for an answer and, later, came to—" Secundus's teeth snapped shut on that revelation.

After a long silence Paulo suggested, "Perhaps you should have agreed."

"It wouldn't have done. She'd have been ruined, never again accepted in Society." Secundus stared over the countryside, his hands unconsciously caressing the old ledge. "Fifteen years," he said so softly Paulo barely heard. He slapped his hand down on the wall. "Enough mawkishness. If that old nancy of a solicitor has the right of it, my family needs me, but I've never been one to take another's word untested, so we'll arrive at the manor tomorrow as if by accident. They needn't think I'm quite on my uppers, of course, but I want a chance to know them before I start paying out my blunt."

"The gelding you bought and the silk we're carrying? They won't give away such a deception?"

"I don't wish to appear destitute, Paulo. Besides, one keeps one's promises if one can, and I promised those things to the children."

Silent again, Secundus wondered if Helen had kept hers. Fifteen years? It was absurd to think she'd be waiting for him. It was a promise he'd refused to accept, asking, *"If I never come back?"* She'd answered, *"Then I'll live a good life some other way. Don't worry about me. I'm not your responsibility until you come home to marry me. But remember, Sec. It's you who thinks we need a fortune."*

Had he been an honorable fool, refusing to run off with his little Helen? Had they wasted fifteen years— good years?

Sec grinned sourly. Why did he persist in such humbug? His Helen was long married and settled into comfortable middle age. She'd be thirty-four now, since he was thirty-nine and she five years the younger. Even if she'd managed, somehow, to stand against her father's wishes and remained unwed, then the likelihood they would still find each other attractive—or even likable— was very close to nil. One changed in fifteen years. Secundus, running a hand through thinning hair, grimaced. At least he hadn't run to fat as Gubby had. Well, tonight they'd stay in Lewes, and tomorrow he'd see about his kin. Then . . . *then* he'd find his Helen. For whatever good that would do.

"You've got yourself into a f-f-fine pickle, haven't you, Gerry?" asked Helen later that same evening when her nephew finished telling her his story.

Gerry laughed. "A very sweet pickle. You will help me, won't you?" he coaxed.

"The Alcesters have a great deal of pride. G-g-giving them anything will require tact." Helen pursed her lips, her eyes narrowing. She tipped her head to one side. "Coal. Hmmm . . ."

"As you say, young Alcester is as proud as he can stare," said John laconically. "I've come up with no idea which wouldn't result in a stiff-necked offer of violence were I foolish enough to carry through the notion."

Helen adopted a smug look. "Well, I've a notion I think will work."

"You do?" asked Gerry and John in unison. "Already?" asked Gerry.

"Surprised? D-d-don't pretend you think me a typical tonish lady with a head full of fluff. Here's what you must do, John. See young Robert and t-t-tell him you require his help. It seems," said Helen, a humorously devious look twisting her features into unusually mischievous lines, "your supplier mistook the order. He delivered far more coal than you need. Robert would be doing you a favor if he'd take it off your hands."

"I give it to him just to be rid of it . . . and he'll accept?"

"Gerry's imp didn't say it was to be a g-g-gift, did she? You offer to sell it. Young Alcester may pay later when he can, of course."

John grimaced. "I see why I didn't find a solution. It never occurred to me to set up as a damn merchant!"

"That takes care of one problem," said Gerry, ignoring the tension between his aunt and uncle.

"But we have others, do we not?" said John a trifle belligerently, because Helen had managed to find a viable solution so quickly, even if it were one he couldn't like. "Helen, my dear, did you remember to buy a new gown for our party?" John rudely looked her up and down, then winced at her ancient brown dress made of a sturdy material which had no other virtue to recommend it. There was a badly mended tear in the skirt, as if she'd cobbled together a rent and never bothered to have her maid fix it properly. The cuffs had been recovered with another, not quite matching, material. "Well? Did you?"

"Th-th-there's plenty of wear in my old yellow."

John's eyes narrowed and his drawl became more pronounced. "Which is five years out of style and was ugly as sin to begin with."

"John, do you or do you not want my services for this p-p-party which you hold each year for no reason other than that our father did so?"

"I need you for my hostess," said Rotherford promptly. He glanced warningly at Gerry, reminding him not to mention the real reason. His sister wouldn't appreciate his efforts to remind her of her proper place in the world or his forcing her to make an appearance in that society.

"Then be still. I'll not spend money on frills I don't need." She shook her head when he opened his mouth. "No, John. I won't allow you to b-b-buy me clothes either. Your choice would make me look a fool, draw attention to me."

"You think the odd things you choose to wear *don't* draw attention? Well, perhaps not," he added. "You've dressed oddly for so long, you're merely thought eccentric and something of a miser." His look softened. "You could look a deal better, Helen."

"For my goals, it is better I don't dress the society matron." Her stammer disappeared when she began discussing her charity work. "The people to whom I wish to speak would have nothing to do with such a woman. If you're in the mood to spend money," she added, a teasing grin returning, "then contribute to one of my funds where the money will be put to good use."

"The sum. I give you each year is more than a pittance."

"Bah! Just a drop in the ocean. Barely a drop. Come with me just once. Follow me through a factory or down into a mine. We'll walk the streets in any of our cities and you'll see the gin-soaked men and women—and children, the poor, poor children—who drink blue ruin to take the edge off the anguish of their lives. Then you'll understand."

Gerry gaped in horror. He hadn't really understood what John had meant about Helen going places she shouldn't. Mines were dangerous. Factories were dirty and dark and had their own dangers. And the slums! He shuddered.

John's rebuttal was, actually, rather a low blow. "If every woman in the ton spent her dress allowance on the poor it would not be enough and, more to the point, you'd add hundreds of sewing girls and abigails to the women now selling themselves on the streets, often not earning enough to keep body and soul together even then, poor creatures." He fisted one hand. "Blast! I wish you'd never gone to that lecture by Elizabeth Fry."

"Dear Elizabeth. She's making plans to help the women prisoners in Newgate," said Helen. John had spoken with more vehemence than ever before. Absently eyeing her brother, she added, "If I could be anywhere near so good a woman as she, I believe I'd become a Plain Quaker myself." John, she thought, was aware of the inadequacy of what was done for the poor. Why, then, did he carp at her for doing what she could?

"Helen, you mustn't spend your capital." He held her gaze when she tried to look away.

Her cheeks reddened. How did he know she'd done so? "I only dip into my principal," she explained, "when I've been unable to raise the money elsewhere."

"If you spent more time raising the money needed for

your projects and less establishing new ones, you'd not find that necessary. Besides, overseeing the schools, kitchens, and orphanages you've already founded must take a great deal of time."

Helen tipped her head, a sad-dog look which stared at nothing at all. She sighed. "John, I p-p-promise I'll think about what you've said. I can't p-p-promise to sit on my hands. I don't know what else I can say."

"Perhaps," said Gerry, trying to lighten what had become much too serious a discussion, "we can find my imp's uncle and ol' Se-cun-dus will have a thing or two to say."

Helen tossed her head and turned toward the hall. "We'll have t-t-to wait and see about Sec, too, won't we? Not that you're likely to locate him, of course. Not after all this t-t-time." She slammed the door behind her.

Gerry and John stared at each other. There'd been a breathless note in Helen's voice which said even more than the slammed door revealed. John scowled. He'd believed Helen had recovered from her infatuation with Secundus Alcester, but it appeared likely he was wrong.

"John," asked Gerry, "did you get the impression Helen knows the Alcester family very well indeed?"

"One did get that feeling, didn't one?" said Rotherford. He went on with less of a dry note, his eyes widening. "I've remembered something. Just a week or so before his death, Helen cornered the captain in the churchyard. She told me she'd given him a piece of her mind, to whit, that if he didn't stop gambling, he'd see his children languishing on the parish." He stared, aghast. "Surely her nagging didn't rip the scales from the captain's eyes."

"You wonder if her lecture caused him to put that gun to his head?"

John moved restlessly in his chair. "It was discovered he'd lost all but one of the farms and the manor house.

But how did Helen know when I hadn't a notion how things stood with him? Not that there is any reason why I should. We didn't run in the same circles, of course."

"Of course," said Gerry in dry imitation. "You know, John, you've gotten awfully starched up."

John shifted uneasily. "Is that the way I sound?"

"High in the instep and arrogant as sin," replied Gerry promptly.

"Gerry, you bought your commission after only half a year at university and helped chase the last French troops out of Spain. You've been out of England ever since, so you've no idea what it's like," said Rotherford a trifle defensively. "I've nearly given up the Season, and I'm very careful when accepting invitations to house parties." Gerry cast him a curious look, so he continued. "It's quite ridiculous, my friend, the measures taken by our sweet, oh-so-innocent, young ladies to get themselves leg-shackled. They'll go any length to trap a man." Gerry tipped his head, questioningly. John smiled ruefully. If relating stories of the embarrassing attempts made to relieve him of his bachelor state would give Gerry's thoughts a new turn, then so be it. "Do let your wise old uncle tell you a tale of *real* danger, Gerry, m'lad. Pay attention, now. I'm about to give you a lesson in the mores and manners of England's most dangerous predator . . . the young and still single female of the species," he added when Gerry's brows rose in query.

The tales John proceeded to tell with all the humor and verve of the true raconteur were quite shocking, and under the laughter Gerry sensed his uncle's disgust with feminine wiles. No wonder John had become a bit of a recluse. The measures taken to force him into marriage were enough to turn most anyone into a cynic, let alone a sensitive man, which John was beneath the cool exterior he'd adopted at a young age.

Later, when the two men picked up their bed candles from the table by the stairs, John thought Gerry rather quiet and wondered if he'd said too much. Gerald was, however, rather ruefully wishing he truly *were* the genie his imp thought him to be. He'd conjure up a loving and generous woman, one just made for his dear old Uncle Hubee. Then he'd do the needful to guarantee they met and fell in love with each other!

Gerry yawned. He was sleepy again, but it was, he realized, a healthy tiredness, and not the uncontrollable need to escape into unconsciousness which had plagued him for so very long. Despite all the things bothering him—the Alcesters and their problems, John's cynicism, and his own nascent desire to put his life back together—he hummed happily as he prepared for bed. Tonight when he went to sleep it would be exactly like any other man seeking his bed, and that was improvement enough for now.

Three

Early the next morning Rotherford rode off to carry out his sister's plan concerning the coal. As he rode up between the ash trees lining the badly-cared-for drive, he saw one of the youngsters in the open doorway. The child paused, turned, and disappeared. John sighed. He'd rather hoped to see Robert Alcester alone. Now he'd be required to do the proper thing by the manor's mistress, whom, for his peace of mind, it would be better to avoid. He dismounted, tossing the reins to the ground. The well-trained eight-year-old, a favorite hack, would happily graze. He gave the animal a final pat and turned.

His heart lurched.

She was framed by the doorway. Wisps of mahogany-colored hair softened the edges of her face. She was tall and didn't bend her knees or slump in an ill-conceived attempt to shorten her magnificent figure to a more fashionable height, as he'd seen tall women do in London. There was intelligence in the eyes she held steadily on his face. For a long moment they stood there, their gaze silently saying things neither was willing to admit aloud. Then Miss Alcester's soft golden skin showed a tinge of pink, and at the same time Rotherford felt his ears heat.

"My lord?" she asked, her normal contralto a trifle high. She cleared her throat. "May I help you?"

Oh yes, he thought. Yes, indeed, you might help, but I can't ask it of you, can I? "I've come to see your brother, Miss Alcester."

"Robert's not here just now, but should return soon. Would you care to wait? Around the side of the house, you'll find a bench and I'll bring you a glass of ale."

"Nothing to drink, thank you." He struggled with his conscience—which told him he should have as little to do with Ruth Alcester as possible—and lost. "Will you keep me company?"

Ruth led the way, making no apologies for the state of the property, the drive which needed graveling, the long grass, the weed-choked flower beds. Ruth Alcester kept her family neat and clean and well fed; her housekeeping was also of the neat and clean variety rather than the prim and polished sort. Rotherford believed she felt it a matter of pride to ignore what could not be cured.

Ruth seated herself, motioning to the other end of the stone bench while attempting to think of something to say. Then she remembered the fish Peter brought home occasionally and a chill settled around her heart. "Is it Peter? About the fish?" she blurted. "Has he been trespassing?"

"Ah ha!" Rotherford suppressed a grin. An excuse had been handed him to postpone deciding how to make the offer of the coal, and he grasped it with both hands. "So he's one of the lads poaching my trout!"

"Trout?" A worried sideways glance didn't reveal the anger she feared. "Peter has brought home nothing so exciting, my lord. But if he and his friends are poaching, which I'll discover soon enough, it'll be stopped."

Rotherford chuckled. "Don't. I'm no fisherman and number none among my friends. I'll make it official, in fact, and talk to my steward . . . although that may ruin half their fun, of course." He lapsed into silence.

After a moment, she said, "Since Robert isn't here,

perhaps you should explain to me what it is you want."
Ruth cast Rotherford another look. It appeared the
baron had some difficulty coming to the point. If he'd
seemed angry—for whatever reason—Ruth could understand the lion of the neighborhood arriving on her
doorstep with the intention of accosting her brother, but
the man didn't. If anything, he seemed embarrassed.

Rotherford dithered. Finally, he said, "I've a problem."

Rotherford had a problem! thought Ruth. An instant's bitterness caused her to wish she might exchange
burdens with him for a week or two.

"My steward thought perhaps your brother might help
us out."

"Certainly, my lord." What was in the wind? "If he can."

"One of my suppliers misread an order. He delivered
next winter's coal and very nearly enough for the following as well. That much extra occupies space I save for
wood, but I don't want to return it since he's never done
such a thing before and I dislike making a fuss of it."
Rotherford shrugged. He slid a glance sideways. Her
face revealed just the reaction he'd expected.

Ruth's smile faded. Her back stiffened into rigidity,
and her features froze into stern lines. "I fail to see
where we can be of aid."

"I rather hoped you might like to buy some of it,"
Rotherford said mildly. "But perhaps I should discuss
this with your brother."

"We have no secrets from each other, my lord." Her
frown didn't lighten. "The problem . . well . . ."

"If you haven't the cash at the moment," he interrupted, "I'm willing to wait for my blunt until you do.
Thing is, if you could take the blasted coal *now,* you'd do
me a favor."

Ruth relaxed. He wasn't offering charity. She disliked
it that he knew they hadn't the money for anything so im-

mediately unnecessary, but that wasn't to be helped. Would life ever become easier? Just enough they needn't worry about every copper spent? *Should* they emigrate as Robert had suggested?

"Well?"

"I must discuss it with Robert, but I'm sure he'll agree."

"To what will I agree?" Robert approached from the back of the house. "Good day, my lord." Rotherford rose to his feet and the men shook hands. The baron explained again. Robert pokered up, until he understood. "I don't know why not."

"Excellent. I'll have it delivered tomorrow if that's not too soon?"

"Have your man leave a bill, my lord," said Robert, on his stiffs again. "I'll settle with your steward as soon as I may."

"No hurry, Alcester. I'm no demmed merchant. And I've no fear you'll renege on the payment," he added when Robert, suddenly thinking a bad harvest might make it difficult, started to change his mind. "You aren't the sort to want the slightest smell of charity about you. The coal will be delivered tomorrow." He waited half a moment for a response before nodding. "We'll see you at the party, of course. Good day, to you." He walked off grumbling, "Helen will have everything at sixes and sevens. Won't be able to call my home my own. Why women must . . ."

Ruth followed Rotherford, drawn by her feelings for him, but Robert simply stared after him. After overhearing criticism of his father as the man gambled away his family's means of livelihood, listening to snide comments and sneers and watching respect fade away, Robert had sworn no one would ever speak so of himself. But how could Rotherford know he felt that way?

Rotherford, meanwhile, realizing Ruth was walking at his side, felt embarrassed. He really must stop talking out loud to himself that way.

"Is Miss Rotherford arrived, then?" asked Ruth. He nodded as they turned the corner, where they found Peter admiring his lordship's mount. Recognizing Rotherford, the boy exhibited a certain wariness, obviously wondering if the baron had learned he and the others fished where they should not. Peter sidled closer to Ruth, glancing up at her and thereby missing the quickly hidden smile the boy's guilty behavior drew to Rotherford's face. Unfortunately, so did Ruth. What she saw was the frown he bent on the boy.

"Well, young man? What do you have to say for yourself, hmmm?"

"I'm sorry," said Peter quickly.

"So, you admit it, do you?"

The lad straightened. "Yes, sir . . . m'lord."

"My lord . . . ," began Ruth, concerned he might have changed his mind.

Rotherford shook his head at her, his eyes silently asking her to let him handle the problem his own way. She closed her mouth, but lay a hand on her brother's shoulder, letting Peter know she was there.

"What do you think should be done with boys who poach?" asked Rotherford, a stern eye on the lad. "Well, Peter?" Rotherford insisted when Peter was slow to answer.

"I don't know, sir . . . m'lord." Peter hung his head.

"You know the law?"

Peter straightened, this time his skin a pale unhealthy color. "Yes, sir . . . m'lord."

"Then you know the danger to yourself and the others."

If it were possible, the boy's color faded still more. "Yes, sir."

"It can't go on." Rotherford paused, eyeing the grim expression aging the lad's face into more mature lines. But the boy didn't cringe; he had exhibited a deal of courage. "Something must be done—did you say something?"

The boy gulped. "No, sir."

Rotherford hid a grin. "Well, *I'll* say this, then: from now on, young Alcester, before you so much as bait a hook, you must find my steward. He'll give you permission to fish my waters. If, for any reason, he tells you no, you go elsewhere. Is it understood?"

Peter met Rotherford's stern gaze, his relief obvious. "Yes, sir."

"Good." Finally Rotherford allowed himself to meet Miss Alcester's eyes. She stared at him, obviously surprised. He smiled, but there was a rueful twist to it. Had she truly thought he'd have the boy transported for nothing more than youthful high spirits? Wishing to stay, wishful to discuss her thoughts and discover if she believed him such an ogre, he very nearly gave in to the temptation. But it would lead, he feared, to more than just talk. The way she sometimes looked at him when she thought he'd not notice indicated that, very likely, she could be lured into just the sort of dalliance he desired of her. But, given who she was, it wouldn't do. "If I hurry," he said, "I'll return in time for breakfast with Helen."

"Give Miss Rotherford my regards, if you'd be so kind, my lord," said Ruth, her voice a trifle uncertain due to the contradictory feelings muddling her. She prodded Peter. The boy thanked Rotherford, bowing with the grace of a young animal. What a good touch he had with Peter, she thought. He'd handled an awkward situation as a lesson rather than simply giving the boy the right to do what he'd been doing illicitly, which would have been far too easy on him. She looked at Rotherford, a warm glow of approval in her eyes. "I thank you as well, my lord. Allowing the boys to fish is very kind of you."

Her look unsettled him. "No such thing," he said a trifle belatedly. "Good day." He gathered up the reins, mounted, and trotted off.

"Ruth," said Peter, jerking on her sleeve, "now we've permission, I should go more often. Fishing, I mean," said Peter urgently. "For the table? Shouldn't I?"

"You must ask Robert. Your work and lessons are more important, are they not? But ask Rob," she finished when the boy's shoulders drooped.

"Rob's being mean. He says I can't. Not for a while."

"Did he say why?"

Peter glowered, then sighed. "He said I made more work for you because I forgot to change my shirt and you had to mend it. But if I fished, they'd be good for dinner, wouldn't they?" He stared with what he obviously hoped was an angelic gaze. Meeting her laughing look, he had the grace to blush.

"I think we'll manage without fish, Peter. What's more, the next time I have to mend something of yours, I'll teach you how to do it."

He glowered. "Girl's work!"

"You think they take girls on board ship to do your mending?" She hid a smile. This was, evidently, a problem which had never before occurred to him.

"Ruth," he said, twisting his toe in the dirt, "Ruth, I'm sorry I made work for you. Maybe," he whispered, "you should teach me to sew on buttons?"

"After dinner we'll find a quiet place and do just that," she agreed. "But you mustn't give up because you find it difficult." He scowled. Ruth knew her younger brother. "Promise me, Peter." He did so with a touch of scorn. "Now you may have until breakfast to tell your friends the new rules about your fishing." She ruffled the boy's hair. Peter ducked from under her hand and, happy again, ran away toward the village.

* * *

Returning to the Hall, Rotherford entered the library. "Well, genie, at grave danger to my peace of mind, the child's first wish has been granted."

"Very good, Hu . . . er . . . John." Gerry grinned. "I'm trying," he insisted, pretending to cower away from the older man's equally mendacious anger. "I remember . . . most of the time. I'll get it yet. No more Hubees. I promise." He couldn't contain his laughter.

"About time," growled Rotherford, secretly delighted at Gerald's teasing. "I'll give orders about the coal and hope young Alcester doesn't see a second delivery coming to the Hall. He was suspicious but too polite to call me on it—stiff-necked young fool."

"I believe you like him."

Rotherford smiled. "Something more must be done to ease their problems." A tremor ran through him as he felt, in memory, the warmth of Ruth's gaze. "Even," he said, pretending indifference, "if it means having that sister stare at me with big eyes."

"Ruth?"

"I believe that's the oldest female's name," he said as if he wasn't sure. "Yes. Ruth Alcester." He turned away. "She does stare, you know. I wonder why."

"Such modesty, John. My imp thinks her sister has chosen the man she wishes to wed. How much would you care to wager it's you with whom she's in love." Gerry pretended sudden enlightenment. "Now there's a solution to all their problems—you should marry her."

"Not me." Rotherford shook his head. It was one thing for him to dream of the lady, but that she dreamed of him? Did that change anything? But no, it wouldn't do. His aunts, all six of them, would have spasms if he married the undowered daughter of a gambler and a suicide.

"If that's the way of it, I refuse to get involved. You, m'boy, must be the means whereby anything else is done. I'll not give Miss Alcester the slightest reason to believe I might return the feeling. Women have a place in one's life, Gerry, but it isn't here at Rother Hall." Was he protesting too much?

Gerry chuckled.

Or not enough? "She's not my sort, Gerry, believe me," said John, earnestly. "Not at all."

Gerry hugged himself, the laughter growing.

Well, in for a pound. . . . Rotherford searched his mind. "Far too tall," he insisted, thinking of long glorious legs. "Far too dark," he added, closing his mind against the notion of gleaming dark hair let down against fair skin. Rotherford shook his head. "I won't give her the least reason to think I might offer for her. Not marriage." Why had he mentioned marriage? "Not so much as a slip on the shoulder," he added.

That last comment stifled Gerald's laughter. "You really have been put off marriage by the machinations you've endured, have you not?"

"I'll marry eventually," said Rotherford blandly. "But I'll not be forced into it by some empty-headed little trickster."

"I understand how you feel, John—given what you told me—but don't put my imp's sister in that category. I won't believe the woman who raised my wee angel could be sly or underhanded."

"Why should I think of her at all?" said Rotherford, every inch a baron.

"Because I find my imp fascinating and don't wish to snub her." Gerry looked up. "I'd have to, wouldn't I, if you took her sister in dislike?"

Had he gone too far in his concern to convince Gerry of his disinterest in Miss Alcester? "You needn't worry. I'll simply have nothing to do with any of them. Yes, Maden?" he added, as his butler entered the room. "Helen's down? Good. I'm sharp set. This doing good deeds must be work. Come along Gerry. One last meal in comfort before my sister turns everything topsy-turvy. We'll be changing for dinner and enjoying all the overrated benefits of civilized behavior, which I don't understand because Helen doesn't run her own household along such formal lines."

"Maybe she's punishing you for making her do what she doesn't want to do," suggested Gerry. Rotherford looked a question. "She said she has no wish to organize your *fête*."

John's eyes opened wide. "Never thought of that. It's just the sort of underhanded revenge Helen would take, isn't it!"

"Well, Paulo?" Paulo didn't answer. The two men had just left the vicar, Mr. Beams, and faced the short ride to the manor—a short ride to a, very likely, emotionally wearing interview with his niece and nephew—Ruth and Robert. And Peter, Elizabeth, and Marie. Why had it never occurred to him his brother might remarry? *Five children.* To what shifts had they been put by his brother's irresponsible behavior?

Secundus climbed up on the seat of the refurbished landau which he'd use until a carriage could be built to his specifications, even though Gubby had denigrated the landau as dowdy. Bless Gubby. Once he'd sorted out his young relatives, he'd invite his friend to visit. If he needed help, Gubby would advise him. No one knew better what was good ton and what was not.

Not that all decisions would be difficult. The boy was sailing-mad. If the lad weren't set on the Royal Navy, he could have a place on the next of Secundus's ships to enter port. Assuming the lad had the character to work and achieve his goals, that is, and assuming the next weren't the *Airy Alice*. He wouldn't place a young boy who must be taught the lot under Captain Mercer.

What of the little girls? Did they have a governess? he'd asked. No, they did not, he was told. He must understand the Alcesters hadn't two sixpence to scratch together. For two years those poor children had scraped and scrimped and kept up appearances mostly from pride alone. If the vicar were to be believed, Robert and Ruth were saints, giving up all chance of a decent life merely to take care of their half brother and sisters. Since Sec didn't believe in real live saints he'd judge for himself. But first he must introduce himself to them. He glanced back at the black gelding with three white stockings, which occasionally danced a bit just from the joy of living. He patted the brown-paper wrapped parcel tied up with string, which held the blue silk he'd brought Ruth, the "dress" he'd promised her. He'd not known of the young ones' existence, but a guinea apiece should make them content.

Paulo turned in between a double row of well-grown ash. Where the trees ended, the drive circled a dry fountain. Beyond that stood a three-story, four-square brick house. Eight windows on each floor winked in the sun, a row of gables making a fourth row along the roof. The front door stood wide, opening to a large and dusky hall where a flight of stairs could be dimly seen. Secundus climbed down. He stood in the sun, listening to the buzzing of bees, remembering long-gone English summers.

He'd come home.

Secundus was still absorbing that notion when a child raced around the corner of the house and slid to a stop. He smiled at her, curious as to which of his young nieces this would be. "Hello," he said.

"Who are you?" She blushed. "Oh dear, that isn't right, is it? I'm supposed to say . . ." Secundus watched her searching her mind, then grinned back when she grinned at him. "I'm supposed to say, 'May I help you?'"

"Yes, you may," he said, warming to the game. "First, tell me your name."

"I am Tibby Alcester, sir, only really that's Elizabeth, but everyone calls me Tibby." She dipped a brief curtsy, looking up at him with a bright, interested gaze. "And you?"

He grinned at her oddly grown-up air. "My name is also Alcester, Miss Alcester. I believe I'm your uncle. You may call me Uncle Sec."

For an instant the child looked faint, and then the lost color returned in a rush. "My uncle, Se-cund-us Alcester?" she asked breathlessly.

"Yes. That's me," he said ungrammatically.

"Oh, that dear sweet genie. I *knew* he'd find you." When her new uncle looked bewildered, she asked, "He did, didn't he? My genie from the lamp." She frowned. "Or was it a bottle?" She brightened. "But he's a good genie, isn't he, even if only a 'prentice." She beamed. "You are one of my wishes."

Sec looked up at Paulo, who looked equally perplexed. "One of your wishes?" asked Sec cautiously.

Tibby was explaining about the coal when Peter arrived on the scene. She broke off to introduce them.

"Uncle? Do we *have* an uncle?" asked Peter suspiciously.

Secundus glanced from one child to the other, from the children back to the open door to the house. What had happened to that sense of homecoming? What *did* he feel? There was the confusion still to be cleared up as to the child and her genie. He'd gotten that far. There was the hilarity he could barely repress at the ruffled feathers and bantamlike behavior of his nephew. And there was Paulo—patient, impassive Paulo. The children whispered. The boy, insisting, grabbed his sister's arm and pinched her.

"Here now!" scolded Sec, humor fading fast. "No gentleman treats a lady like that. Peter, is it? You'll never make a decent officer if that's the way of it!"

Peter's face flamed. "I'm older and she should mind me, but she won't."

"Not if what you say is foolish," pouted the child. "I will *not* run for Robert. Our uncle is not trying to put one over on us. We do too have an uncle."

"Then why have I never heard of him? Why have we never met him? If he's been gone, then why didn't he write us, and why didn't he come when he knew our father died?" Peter stood, legs apart, head back, his hands fisted into his hips. His expression dared Secundus to explain . . . if he could.

"I haven't a notion why you've never heard of me. It is none of your business why I never wrote. And I came as soon as I knew Primus was dead. India, my boy, is not a hop, skip, and a jump down the road."

A bit of Peter's antagonism evaporated, but not the suspicion. "It only takes six months to India. It's been two years."

"I got the letter from your father's solicitor—when was it, Paulo?"

"Five months, three weeks, and two days. We were near Benares on the Ganges when the letter reached you, second son of your honored father."

Tibby, who had shown no fear before, slid nearer her uncle and reached for his hand. "He talks," she whispered.

"Yes," Sec whispered. "He does."

Peter ran into the house and back out. Following more slowly was a tall young woman, her dark hair wound into a loose knot on the top of her head. She was drying her hands on an apron. Secundus recognized the family traits in her features, and that feeling of being home returned with a rush. "You must be Ruth," he said, softly.

"Uncle Secundus?" For a moment she seemed uncertain, and then her face lit with a welcoming smile, dimples coming into play, her hands held out to him. "It is! I don't think you've changed a bit except to catch the sun. Why, we spoke of you just the other night, I can't *believe* this. Peter, find Rob. And Marie. Where is Rob? But, I'm forgetting my manners. Do come in. Are you thirsty? Oh dear. I'm still the featherhead, am I not? Would you introduce me . . . ?"

Before her uncertainty became too obvious, Secundus drew Paulo forward. "This is Paulo da Silva, my friend, who has saved my life more than once—most recently aboard ship when I was more than a little ill."

"Honored Alcester is too kind, Miss Alcester." The Goan bowed. "I am no more than a poor secretary who would die for this brave man who has saved *my* pitiful and useless life several times over."

Ruth blinked. "You are too modest, sir," she said. "My uncle says you are his friend. Please be generous and allow us to be your friends, too."

Secundus released a silent breath of joy. He looked to see if her sister's acceptance of Paulo eased Tibby's uncertainty about the stranger. Tibby had her lip between her teeth, worrying over Ruth's words. Suddenly she moved forward and held out her hand. "Would you like to see our home?"

"I'd like that very much," said Paulo just as seriously.

As an excuse to hide moist eyes, Secundus turned to the carriage. The gelding, still tied at the back, was restless. "Can I put the beasts in the pasture?" he asked Ruth. She helped him unhitch before they, too, went inside.

Tibby was still explaining to Paulo. "But mostly we live in the kitchen, because it's warm from the cooking and we save fuel." The child opened the door at the back of the hall, went down a short passage, down three steps, and into the kitchen. "We do most of our work here." Secundus, following, peered around the low-beamed room. No cook. Not even a scullery maid. Had they no servants at all? he asked.

"We've a woman who comes in occasionally to do the heavy work," Ruth told him.

"I'll do something about that soon enough," he muttered.

The back door opened and Peter, still suspicious, burst in, Robert following close behind.

"Uncle Alcester?"

"Uncle Sec well do. You're Robert?"

"Yes, sir."

"We'll have a long talk soon, boy, but at the moment I simply want to get to know you all." In the getting to know each other, Secundus lost sight of the fact there were no servants. He was drawn into telling stories of his life in India, the younger children—even Peter—sitting on the floor near him and hanging on each and every word. Robert, too, sat silent through the tales, as enthralled as the little ones at hearing, firsthand, about a country which was as much a mystery as was fairyland.

Paulo refused to join them at table, where Ruth eventually laid out their dinner, but proceeded to prepare his own food. "Tomorrow we will begin lessons and you may teach me to cook your food," Ruth said.

"Tomorrow," said Secundus, sternly, "we hire a cook and a maid and a footman and—I forget what's needed in a decent English house."

"A *mali*," said Paulo from where he measured rice into boiling water.

"Of course. A *mali*. A gardener should be among the first we hire."

Ruth and Robert stared at each other. "Sir . . . ," began Robert.

"Not a word. If I weren't such a stubborn damn—" he met Tibby's wide-eyed gaze, and a dot of red darkened his tanned checks, *"dratted* fool," he amended, "I'd have been here when you needed me. Servants' wages won't make a dent in my pocket. Don't think it. You youngsters need someone to look after you, and, by Old Nick's knickers, I'll do it if it takes my last bit of blunt. Not that it will," he added, rubbing his nose.

Late that night, his mind too active to drop off to sleep, Sec reviewed the day. The children. Tibby had thanked him prettily for the guinea he'd given her and then, gently, urged shy Marie to do likewise. Even Peter had lost another ounce of suspicion when given a gift. Peter needed a stronger hand, perhaps, and Marie would never be more than a sweet and harmless nodkin, but Tibby was something else agan! Ruth and Robert were grown-up versions of the children he recalled—no surprises there.

Servants. He'd sort that out first thing. It was as well he'd gone overboard when ordering from London purveyors of tea, coffee, and wine. He'd also chosen several hams and a variety of cheeses—he'd missed having cheese while in India. There were other things, too, but having delicacies of an elegant nature weren't needed so much as brick and mortar and timbers for general repair. Paulo would discover what was needed of that sort.

Helen. He drew in a deep breath and let it out slowly. Helen, *Miss* Helen *Rotherford,* was visiting at the Hall. She wasn't married. What other surprises might he find concerning his Helen? Oh, how he longed to see her again, his plump little robin, his little blue-stocking with the little stammer which disappeared when she spoke of things of interest to her. Had she continued to enlarge her mind? Had she established and run a charity for orphans as she'd suggested she might do? Or had her father forced her to conform to Society's dictates?

What would he find when he found the courage to reintroduce himself to his love? Tomorrow maybe? Would she even remember him, or remembering, would it be as anything more than an acquaintance? Would he like the woman she'd become, or had he been coveting a dream all these years?

Sec sighed. He'd been over and over these notions. Soon he'd see his Helen. When he did, he'd discover the answers. Until he did, he must put such useless speculation from his mind and go to sleep.

Four

Helen looked up from the letters forwarded by her secretary. Rarely did anyone dare disturb her when she adjourned to the small parlor she'd appropriated for an office. She wondered what disaster brought Maden to break into the private afternoon hour on which she insisted.

"Yes, Maden? Is C-C-Cook threatening to leave? Or have they sent word from Brighton the marquees we ordered are unavailable? No, the purveyors of tents would contact my brother. It must be Cook."

Maden, a faintly scornful look on his long, narrow face, stalked forward, extending a salver on which lay a white card, the corner bent to indicate its owner had himself called. Hesitantly, Helen picked it up and sent him an accusing glance. He bowed his silver-topped head, but refused to explain.

Helen lay aside her pen and lifted her quizzing glass. Maden was one of the few people to whom she admitted her eyes were inadequate for many tasks. She'd tried spectacles, but was forever losing or breaking them. Besides, in her estimation, they made her ugly. At thirty-four Helen was no longer young, but she was not *old*, and had, she'd discovered, more vanity than was very likely proper.

Her color fluctuated alarmingly. Secundus. Here. Now.

She drew in a deep, steadying breath. "Maden," she said, setting aside the card, "I assume you've a reason for bringing this to me? Now? During my private time?" He bowed. "You think I should see him?" Again Maden bowed. "It's been years, Maden." This time he nodded.

Helen pursed her lips, drawing in a deep breath through her nose. She stared out the window, her mind, whether she willed it or no, drifting back to a day very like this. He'd been determined. She'd been flighty and perverse. He'd become angry and told her he'd not come to her until he was the wealthy man her father insisted she wed.

"I'll see him." Maden bowed and started for the door. "But not here." The butler paused and, hands folded, waited. "Oh blast and bedamned, I'll do it," she said mysteriously. "Wait a few minutes and send him to the Lady's Garden. He'll know." She wondered, belatedly, if Secundus *would* remember. Well, they'd see, wouldn't they?

Helen went directly to the center of a convoluted pattern of ancient walks protected by high hedges. They'd been planted nearly a century earlier as a place where ladies might exercise protected from the wind, and had grown into something of a maze. She seated herself on a bench outside the vine-covered pavilion. Once settled, she opened a book—careful to hold it right side up, having once been caught with one upside down. She heard steps on the raked gravel, but waited to look up until her visitor reached the arched trellis, the entrance to the center of the maze. Sec stood framed by the roses climbing over it. Her eyes met his. Neither said a thing for a long moment.

"Well, Secundus?"

"Is it well?" he asked softly, more than a trifle diffidently. He studied her, liked what he saw.

Helen had reduced her excessive plumpness long ago

and didn't consider that he might see changes in her. She was too busy noting a mismatched button on his vest where someone—Ruth, probably—had been unable to find one like the others. She stared at his thinning hair and old-fashioned queue. Her eyes flitted to his scuffed boots. "I tr-tr-truly thought you'd return to England only as a nabob," she said.

"While I truly believed you married before I reached India."

"You wronged me." She felt the embers of a resentment she'd not realized smoldered within her.

"I overestimated your father. He had that match arranged for you."

Match? Bewilderment smothered a bit of the fire. "What match? There was no match. Did *he* tell you such a clanker?"

"Your brother told me when I asked him to bring you that last message."

"John? *John* told you?" John? Had he? How dared he! Surely not. "He was only a boy."

"With all the Rotherford pride." Sec grimaced. "I promised I was saying goodbye. It was the only way he was going to agree to give you the note."

That added fuel to her smoldering indignation. "I t-t-told you I'd marry no one but you."

"I told you I couldn't, wouldn't, hold you to me when I couldn't promise to return for you."

"Whose pr-pride spoke then?"

A smile twisted Sec's lips. "Mine."

They stared at each other. "Have we lived long enough to get beyond pride, Secundus?" she asked quietly.

"I'd like to try." He rubbed his nose. "However, I was gone a bit longer than need be"—neither blinked at the understatement —"since you were never wed. I don't see how you can forgive that," he said softly.

She noted the wary look in his eyes and gnashed her teeth. "Don't be a f-f-fool, Sec. I'd have married you when we'd barely a guinea between us. Why should I care if you've returned no richer than when you left? Especially when I've my inheritance and am quite wealthy now."

"I've a few pice to call my own," he said blandly.

"P-p-pice?"

"An Indian coin of small value. All I meant was I'm not destitute."

"All the better." He still didn't come to her, stood quite still, waiting for something. She didn't know what, however. "I don't w-w-wish to push you into anything, of course."

"Nor I you," he said in a rush. "I think we should take it slowly this time. Get it right."

Surprise touched her. He was correct, of course. Fifteen years had passed. Neither of them was the person they had been. Even though none of the feeling was gone, still, there was a sense she didn't quite know this man for whom she'd waited, longed, for so many years. "Yes. I see. Yes, perhaps we should go on as we are, each in our own place. Time will tell us if we wish for more from each other."

"I'll tell you now, Helen, I haven't changed." He noted her wary look. "My feelings, I mean."

"Nor mine," she said quickly, adding, "but we've both done much, seen much, in the passing years, have we not? I would wish to know we can support each other's ambitions in life before we go further."

He took a closer look at his Helen. "But can I support you, I wonder? Keep you up to the mark?" he teased. Even he knew the dress she wore was out of date. He decided she was exactly to his tastes. "I'd not like to think you might be reduced to the secondhand clothes barrows, my Helen."

Helen knew he was asking why she looked a dowd, and, forgetting he had no business talking about her clothing when dressed so poorly himself, she bridled. "I c-c-cared little enough for such stuff, back then, when every girl d-d-dreams a little. Since then, Sec, I spend every pence I can raise helping the poor. I'd better make that clear before we go one step further." She sighed. "You'll see me here at the Hall in the midst of great gaiety, but that's not the life I lead, Sec. I don't wish to mislead you."

Secundus thought back to the garden parties he'd known, the stiff formal manners, a bored host, subdued children in their best clothes. What gaiety?

"I've given the years to organizing orphanages, kitchens—whatever is needed, and then, of course, supporting them is a whole separate problem."

As Helen talked about her projects, her features lightened with the charm Sec recalled. As always when she allowed her tongue freedom, her enthusiasm glowed through every word, and the delightful stutter he found so touching disappeared. Her intelligence shone and her effervescent smile came and went. Long ago Secundus had fallen in love with the woman he'd believed she'd become; now she proved he'd been right, and he found himself falling in love all over again—if he'd ever stopped loving her—which he doubted. She faltered and, faintly embarrassed, stopped speaking, her questioning gaze meeting his.

"You've done well, m'love. I'd like to help you if there's anything I can do," he said gently.

"Would you Sec? Would you?"

"Only let me get my family in order, and we'll run off together for the last time," he said, tongue in cheek.

"*Secundus*," she scolded, her eyes lighting at his teasing, "you promised you'd never ever mention that old foolishness."

"I haven't," he grinned. "I only mentioned the next time."

"*I'd* have gone through with it, if you'd not been so idiotishly noble." Helen pouted in a way she'd have stigmatized as flirtatious in another.

Sec touched her lips gently. "Coming to my rooms that evening—it was the most idiotic thing you ever did, m'love. I wondered if you'd fallen in love with the man I thought you knew me to be, or with some dream figure you'd made up. You should have known I'd not allow you to ruin yourself."

"I was desperate."

"So was I. Do you think it was easy, taking you home, helping you slip back in?" Secundus closed his eyes against remembered pain. "The temptation to head north to Gretna Green was very nearly more than I could bear."

"I'm glad you were at least tempted. Sometimes, you see, I wondered." Helen hooked her arm through his and strolled toward the arch. "But enough old history. T-t-tell me, how is Ruth? I've just got home and not had time to see her yet, but I've the wish to do so. Do tell me what you've done so far for the children. Maybe I can help you there."

Rotherford, deep creases marring his usually impassive features, rose from the seat inside the pavilion where, his concentration on the *Edinburgh Review* broken, he'd been an inadvertent eavesdropper. He stared at the empty arch. Had he ever, he wondered, known his sister? Helen had actually tried to elope with that man? And now, was Alcester seriously suggesting they carry through the notion?

Obviously Alcester had *not* made a fortune in India or surely he'd have said so. Having found Helen still infatuated with him, did he intend to repair that omission by marriage? Damnation. He'd interfered once and erred. Dare he interfere again? But didn't he have an obligation to protect his sister if the man were nothing but a fortune hunter?

John recalled his last conversation with Alcester. Helen's suitor had treated him as an adult, had tried to give the boy he'd been a deeper understanding of Helen. He'd insisted she'd be destroyed if their father succeeded in turning her into the sort of Society matron of which he approved—into the image of their father's favorite, their older sister, Gerry's mother, who had died.

John shook his head as he remembered the scorn with which he'd listened to the down-at-heels suitor. As time passed he'd discovered how seriously Helen took her work. *Now* he understood, but at the time he'd been certain of the rightness of his father's demands.

John didn't understand what he was feeling. It upset him to discover the strange emotion was shame. He should have favored the pair. Helen had had some money, even before their father's death—enough to support them in comfort if not elegantly. The couple had wasted the past fifteen years. Shame was a sensation formerly unknown to him.

John's lips twisted in a wry way that lacked humor, and a bark of sardonic laughter escaped him. His next interview with Alcester should be interesting. First, he must apologize for his attitude in the past and, then, having admitted he'd made a mistake *then*, he had to determine if the man Alcester had become was good enough for Helen *now*. It would be truly ironic if, having decided the much younger Alcester should have been allowed Helen's hand, he discovered the older man had been hardened by experience. He wondered if he could pull it off without embarrassing either himself or Alcester. Then he wondered why he worried about embarrassment. His sister must be protected and he'd see she was, but deep in his heart he hoped all would be well for her this time.

A further thought caused his throat to tighten: say Alcester *was* no longer good enough for Helen. Warning the man off, he must then avoid the man's family—in particular, his niece, Miss Alcester. He must stop allowing himself even that one dance with her at parties they both attended, stop his furtive observation of her when they happened to be in the same place. He'd have to put her from his mind altogether.

Now, why did that conclusion hurt so much? Admitting to one new emotion had been hard. Rotherford refused to face a second.

When Tibby found her genie by the pond she twirled in a circle. "Oh, genie, you did it! Thank you so much. It was 'ficient of you to do it that way, wasn't it?"

"Did what, Tibby? What did I do efficiently?"

"Found our uncle, of course. You said you couldn't, and then you did and he gave Ruth material—such a be-u-tiful blue—for a gown, and Robert a horse. That's what I mean, 'ficient. The coal, too. That's come already. I think you like to tease me," she scolded.

"Tibby, back up. Your uncle has come home?"

"You're still teasing," she said, but with less certainty.

"I don't like to disappoint you, Tibby, but I had nothing to do with his arrival. Nothing whatever. But that isn't important, is it? What's important is that he's here and he'll help you." Gerry tipped his head, inquiringly. "He is willing to help, isn't he?"

"Yes. He'll get us a cook and a maid and a . . . a *mali.*" When Gerry looked confused, Tibby added, "That's what they call a gardener in India. Ruth won't have to work her fingers to the bone, and Robert will have time to play with us and—oh, I don't know. All sorts of good things."

"Maybe he'll get a governess for little girls who listen at doors so they'll learn it isn't the proper thing to do."

Tibby pouted at the reprimand. Then she stared at him. Defiantly. "If I *hadn't* listened, how would I know what to wish for?" she defended herself.

"You shouldn't know such things. You're just a little girl."

Stubbornness tilted her chin. "It's my family. I want to help."

"The thing is, Tibby," he said gently, "you're too young to help."

"But I *did* help. I catched you and I didn't waste my wishes."

Gerry sighed. It was past time to stop this nonsense. The question was, how did one disillusion such a generous little imp? Still, she mustn't think wishing brought one things. Fairies and leprechauns did not exist. Certainly not genies out of lamps! "Tibby . . ." He held out his hand and Tibby put her own into it. He still couldn't think what to say. Finally he simply blurted the truth. "Tibby, I'm not really a genie."

"You explained that. You're only a 'prentice." She patted his hand.

"You don't understand, child. I lied. You caught me half awake, and I thought it was a game, so I went along with it. I pretended to be what you thought me to be, but I didn't have a thing to do with your wishes coming true." He squeezed her hand gently. "Will you be my friend even if I am only a man?"

Tibby hesitated. "You wanted to make me happy, didn't you?"

"I wanted to make life easier for you. But it's a game

that must go no further. You didn't know it was a game, Tibby, and that was wrong of me."

Tibby thought about that. "It was rather nice having my very own genie."

"Even only an apprentice genie?"

"Yes. Even only a 'prentice genie." Tibby stood up. "I've got to go now. I told Ruth I wouldn't be long." Tibby started away, turning back just where the path curved, that trace of a frown back. "Will I see you again now that you're not my genie?"

"You'll find me here most days, Tibby. It's peaceful and pleasant."

She brightened. "You want me to come?"

"You're a very special little girl. I'll be unhappy if you *don't* come."

Her smile widened. "'Bye. I'll come soon."

But would she? Her newfound uncle might have notions about allowing the child to roam all by herself. Gerry shrugged. He lay back, gazing at the clouds and thought about Tibby and what a nice child she was. It seemed life still held something of interest after all. Gerry savored the feeling as he soaked up the healing rays of the sun.

That evening Gerry told Helen that Secundus Alcester had returned home. "So." Her brows rose but she hid a smile. "You've d-d-discovered my Secundus is h-h-home." After a moment she turned to stare at her brother. "Well, John? Will you interfere as you did before?"

Rotherford thought of evading the issue, but decided that it was best to face it. "Alcester promised without my asking that he was saying goodbye."

"Which is all the b-b-blasted man did. Not even one kiss to remember him by." Helen's face twisted in regret. She shook her head slowly from side to side. "Fifteen years he's been gone. Do you think we'll even like each other now he's come home to me?"

"You'll have to decide that, won't you? I don't suppose I'll interfere now," he said nonchalantly and inaccurately, "but what makes you believe he's not married?" Rotherford tossed and caught the faceted crystal top to the decanter. Would she admit she and Secundus had already met and talked?

"He isn't married," asserted Helen.

She was so certain that Gerry, who didn't know of the morning visit, blinked. "Wait a moment. Helen, is that why you never married? Do you and my imp's uncle have an understanding?"

"No." She scowled at her brother. "He was far too honorable to agree to a secret engagement or even to an exchange of letters for which I also begged. Great Caesar's ghost, I'd no pride at all, had I? Since my brother, who was too young to know, and my father were against the match, Sec insisted I must be free. But he's never married," she said smugly. "I know."

Gerry pursed his lips. She didn't know. Couldn't know. "You didn't marry," he said slowly. Was that why she thought he hadn't?

"Not for lack of offers," John said softly.

"Offers!" Helen whirled away and back. "Oh yes!" Her anger could be felt, vibrating clear across the room. "Offers for the Rotherford money I'd bring with my fat and stuttering self. N-n-no one but my dear Secundus ever saw the p-p-person inside. Not one of them."

"You're not fat," said Gerry.

His aunt smiled at him. "Thank you. Not that it matters anymore."

"It no longer matters whether Alcester still wishes to marry you?" he asked, daringly pretending to misunderstand.

Helen's tone was defensive when she responded, "I

m-m-meant it no longer m-m-matters that all the offers I received were from fortune hunters."

"So," suggested John, tossing the decanter top once more, still wishing she'd tell them of the visit, "if Alcester comes by one day soon and asks my permission to approach you, I'm to tell him no?"

Helen closed her eyes and drew in a slow breath. She let it out equally slowly. "Gerry, has it ever o-o-c-c-curred to you John draws the oddest conclusions from a p-p-perfectly clear sum of information?"

"You mean my Tibby's uncle is not a fortune hunter?"

"Of course he is not, but that isn't what I meant."

"Then you mean John is not to show Alcester the door if Maden allows him to cross the threshold?"

She grinned, her mood lightening. "When dear old Maden shows my Sec in, we needn't worry. He'll not let *John* know about it."

"You think my butler has more loyalty to you than to me?" Having asked the question, it occurred to John that obviously Maden had. The butler was another who had not mentioned Alcester's morning visit.

"Maden was always on my side. Often and often, when we first met, Maden would send Sec around to the Lady's Garden. We got to know each other very well that month before the Season began and we went up to London."

"*How* well?" asked John sharply. "You were unchaperoned!"

"John," said Helen patiently, "do you think Maden would have allowed any young man near me if he hadn't judged the man honorable and trustworthy?"

A muscle in John's cheek jerked. "I don't like it."

"What business of yours is it that I enjoyed several tête-à-têtes with Secundus about which you knew nothing? John, you were fifteen at the time."

"You were and are my sister, dammit."

"Language, language!"

"Helen . . ."

"As you pointed out, I'm no longer a girl. I am not foolish. And I will not do anything I'll regret. Does that settle the nonsense running around the mind one presumes you must have?"

The muscle twitched again. "I did say I'd not interfere, didn't I?"

"You did."

"Now how did I come to do anything so foolish?" And how was he to discover the facts he needed concerning Secundus Alcester? He tossed the top to the decanter a third time, fumbled it, and, as he picked it up, it occurred to him the best source of information concerning Alcester was Alcester's family. He could ask Miss Alcester. "Brandy, Gerry?" he asked before Helen could respond to his rhetorical question. "You, Helen?"

Rotherford served Gerry and himself with brandy and his sister with a light sherry, then, deliberately, he turned the conversation to the proper organization of workhouses. When he'd accepted the position of trustee and looked into the functioning of the local institution, he'd discovered several problems. He wanted Helen's advice on changes he thought necessary. His authority as trustee gave him the power, but he'd decided to do nothing precipitously. Now seemed an ideal time to bring it up; not only did he truly wish to know Helen's views, but he also wished very much indeed to avoid any more talk of Secundus Alcester. And, having discovered a legitimate excuse—or perhaps rationalization—for seeking out Ruth, he didn't wish to think about *that* either.

A few days later, Ruth looked around the kitchen which was no longer her province. Mrs. Blough produced fine meals with the most meager of supplies, but she hated having anyone around while she did it. Ruth heard her sniff, took the hint, and returned to the hall where she had to sidestep to avoid the new footman industriously rubbing wax into the paneling.

Upstairs Mary sang as she worked. The maid was only fifteen, but she came from a large family and had informed Ruth—who had suggested she was trying to do too much—that working at the manor was easy. She loved her new duties and her mama had promised she could have a whole shilling each quarter just for herself. It was a generous offer. Many girls in service sent home all of their wages. Mary wouldn't approve her mistress helping with the everyday work.

So what was she to do? This was ridiculous. She'd never lived a boring day in her life. But she was bored.

There was no question about it! The only thing of interest on her horizon was the garden party—for which she needed a dress. She had the silk Secundus gave her but no notion what to do with something so fine. Lucy Chalmers would know. And Lucy had a knack for cutting patterns. She'd take the material to Lucy.

An hour later Ruth handed the old cob over to a Chalmers groom. She asked him about his niece who had gone into service and was told the girl had a fine position in the city. The front door stood open, welcoming, and Ruth entered. No one was about so she hallooed.

Squire himself came into the hall. "Miss Alcester," he said politely.

"Mr. Chalmers. How are you? I've come to impose on Lucy if she isn't too busy. I've a beautiful piece of material, and there is no one I'd trust as I trust Lucy to help me cut it."

The squire cleared his throat. He hemmed. He hawed. Finally, embarrassed, he told her Lucy was up in her bedchamber. The squire scowled fiercely. "My daughter is the most stubborn child a man could ever have."

Ruth winced at the glare he threw her way. Her back straightened. "Speak plainly, Mr. Chalmers."

"You want plain speaking, miss, you may have it. She's in her room and refuses to come out. That blasted brother of yours has turned my girl's head, and she's neither to drive nor to lead!" But the gray-haired man looked more bewildered than angry. "I won't have her living as you do."

It was Ruth's turn to glare. "Robert loves Lucy very much—too much to ask such sacrifice of her. You do him a disservice if you blame him or think he encourages her. He doesn't."

The squire deflated like a punctured bladder. His shoulders drooped and his eyes shifted around the hall. He was, after all, a just man. "I know. I know. But, the Chalmers have held this property for four hundred years, Miss Alcester. And Lucy must do her duty by it. Why can't she understand that?"

Ruth swallowed the words she nearly blurted out in favor of her brother. They would do no good. The squire didn't object to Robert, the man, but to Robert's lack of fortune. He'd mentioned the Chalmers's long tenure on the land, but not their equally long tradition of marrying well!

"Lucy's being punished?" she asked.

"That's not the way of it at all," growled Mr. Chalmers. "Not at all. I merely told her I didn't wish to see her face until she'd come to her senses." His lips pursed, pressing together and relaxing several times. "I don't understand the chit and that's the truth."

"Do you object if I go up to her?"

"No, no objection to *you*." Squire almost met her eyes, flicked his look toward the vase of drooping flowers set on the hall's side table. He harrumphed. "Might see if

you can talk some sense into her—if you'd be so kind."
He cleared his throat. His color rose. "Can't seem to find
anything. Can't seem to stomach the food either. Place
needs her hand to the plow, you might say." He sent a
pleading look her way. "Might just ask how long she's
going to sulk?" he asked on a hopeful note.

"No," said Ruth. Mr. Chalmers gave her a sharp, narrow-
eyed, glare. "I won't do that for you, sir. I don't think it's
fair to ask it of me."

Ruth held his gaze, and the squire's ruddy complexion darkened still more. "No," he decided. "Not fair.
Young Alcester's sister, after all. Sorry."

"I'll just run up and see if she'll help me, shall I?"

"Very well. Go on up with you. Go on up." He stared
at the dying flowers. As he watched, a head of petals
sifted down to lie in the dust. He moved slowly out the
door, looking very unhappy.

Ruth watched him go before starting up the stairs.
Lucy peered out of the sitting room attached to her bedroom. Ruth smiled at the questioning look on her
friend's face.

"Is he gone?" whispered Lucy.

"Not far, I think." Ruth tipped her head. "What happened, Lucy?"

"He said I was to wed a proper man. I said it was
Robert or no one. He said he didn't wish to see my face
until I came to my senses." Miss Chalmers's chin firmed
stubbornly. "It'll be long and long before I see his sort of
sense, but enough of my problems. I heard something
about material, I think?" Lucy stared inquisitively at the
brown-paper covered package.

"The most beautiful silk I've ever seen," said Ruth. "I
want a new gown for the party. Will you help me?" Ruth
hugged the parcel.

Lucy took one look at the blue silk and pronounced it

far too fine for a garden party. She insisted she'd not be attending the *fête* and that it would please her if Ruth would allow the gown she'd made for herself to be altered to fit Ruth's much taller figure. "Truly, I won't attend the party, so at least try it on?" she coaxed.

Ruth couldn't resist trying it. It was the prettiest thing she's worn in years. "I can't take it, Lucy. Your father . . ."

"Don't say a word, Ruth." Lucy held up her hand, admonishingly; her chin rose and her pretty little mouth thinned. "I know my father will have asked you to do so, but . . ."

"He asked me to find out how long you'd go on sulking, and I told him I'd do no such thing," said Ruth pacifically, staring at her reflection.

"Good for you. But you think I should go to the party, do you not?"

"Not that you must, but, Lucy, how can you bear to miss it?"

"Miss a chance to see Robert, you mean?" Lucy's grin faded. "Missing a party is nothing. What I will not miss is my whole life."

"Lucy, do you think you *can* change your father's mind?"

"I must. I can't go on, always hoping for a glimpse of Robert, for a word with him. I understand why he thinks he mustn't ask for my hand, but I'll never be happy with anyone else. Father thinks it girlish nonsense which I'll get over," Lucy finished bitterly.

"You'll make yourself ill, Lucy," said Ruth, concerned.

"When Father is gone, I go out for exercise. But I do nothing else." Lucy grinned. "Mrs. Woods hasn't a notion about a proper menu. I don't order supplies or oversee the housekeeping. I don't keep the books. I don't—"

"Do the flowers," interjected Ruth with a smile.

"Do they need changing? Oh, dear," said Lucy with

false concern, "I suppose it's occurred to no one to throw out old bouquets and make up new." When they stopped laughing, Lucy said, "I love him dearly, but I'll not be used as a pawn in his plans for a grand marriage." She shrugged. "Take the dress, Ruth. Please. Lord Rotherford would like how you look in it," she added slyly.

Ruth, blushing, touched the material and her rough skin caught on a thread. She sighed. "Oh, Lucy, even if I *were* to wear it, I'd look a guy."

"You've two weeks. I'll give you a jar of my hand cream, and you may buy lotion in the village for your face."

"If you've extra made up, I'll gladly accept something which will help my poor hands." Ruth gazed sadly at her reflection. "As to buying something for my complexion, I can't. The only money in the house belongs to Tibby—gifts to her. She told me to keep her guineas for 'mergencies.'"

"So tell her it's an emergency. You need to fade your freckles." Lucy giggled when Ruth whirled to peer into the mirror.

"Lucy Chalmers, that was mean. I thought you'd actually seen freckles!"

Lucy grinned. "If you can't buy Denmark Lotion, I'll give you some lemons. The juice is very good for fading sun-touched skin."

"Hail to ye, ye ol' wise woman," intoned Ruth, giggling. "I'll take the lemons, thank you. Not that I'll become pale and interesting in the time available. But not," she added and reached for the hooks, "the dress. It's lovely, Lucy. You'll look beautiful at the party," she hinted.

"I thought that settled. Leave those hooks alone until I see how much to add at the bottom. Ruth, believe me," she added, catching Ruth's busy fingers, "I'll not attend the party." She rolled her eyes toward the skies. "I'll be learning off by heart another set of verses from *Childe Harold.*"

"Doing *what?*"

"Father detests poetry. Every time he pauses outside my door, listening to see what I'm up to, I quote off a few pages. Now, a five-inch ruffle set just here, I. . . ." She glanced up. "Oh, Ruth, Rotherford will like it, believe me." Ruth, who had never admitted even to Lucy her infatuation, bit her lip and turned away. "Silly Ruth," Lucy giggled. "Or perhaps it's that I'm in love myself that I know how you feel."

After a pause Ruth sighed softly. "It's so hopeless, isn't it?"

"And aren't we a pair of simpletons for dreaming after the impossible?"

The two sat down side by side on Lucy's bed and, simultaneously, sighed.

Five

While Ruth wended her way home thinking she'd gone from not having enough hours in her day for all that needed doing, to having so many it seemed impossible to find ways to fill them, Secundus cornered Peter concerning his wish to go to sea. Soon he was explaining what would be expected of the boy.

"Lessons!" Peter looked at his uncle aghast. "The captain will supervise my *lessons?*"

"Certainly." Secundus, facing the indignant lad's outrage, restrained a strong desire to laugh. "It's his duty."

"But I want to be a sailor," said the boy, "not a scholar."

"I assume you wish to become an officer?" Secundus looked down his nose at his distressed nephew. "Eventually?"

"Of course."

"Do I hear scorn, young man?" Peter continued to wear a belligerent look. "Officers are gentlemen, m'boy. Educated gentlemen."

"Just to sail a ship from one place to another?"

"How ignorant the young can be," mused Secundus aloud. "Peter, have you the imagination to visualize being surrounded by water? Nothing but water in all directions? No hills. No trees. No roads to follow to the nearest signpost?" Peter nodded slowly. "Now think of a storm. To save the ship and your worthless life, you must run with the wind, not fight it." Peter nodded more sharply, his eyes glowing with excitement. Remembering his own reaction to rough seas, Secundus repressed a shudder. "All right, you've run with the wind and the wind has finally blown itself out. Now. Where are you?"

Peter looked bewildered. "What do you mean, where am I?"

"How do you know how far off course you are? Perhaps the ship is damaged and you must put into port for repairs. Where is the nearest one? Remember, you are in the middle of an ocean. There are no landmarks."

Peter looked thoughtful. "There's a way to figure it out?"

"I'm no sailor, Peter, nor do I wish to be. But hear me well, m'lad, when it's necessary for me to board a ship, I hope the officers are a lot better educated than you appear to be." Secundus didn't hide a sneer. In actual fact, he exaggerated it since, somehow, he must get through to the boy.

Peter's skin turned bright red. "Robert tried to tell me. . . . It didn't seem like much, making the ship go. The wind does it." Peter scuffed his toe into the grass. "I'm learning to sew," he said.

"Very good. If you bring that ship to shore, you may stay and set up as a tailor. So what should you learn, you ask? The things any gentleman learns. Latin, Greek, history. You must know the globes and how to use them. Mathematics. Particularly mathematics. Now," he continued before Peter could comment, "are you set on the Royal Navy? Perhaps I can get you on a ship of the line, but it would be easier if you'd settle for a commercial vessel."

Peter's eyes widened when he realized what he was being offered. *"Anything!"* Peter tugged at his uncle's arm. "Please. I promise to never complain about the

stupid lessons. I'll do anything if only I can go to sea."
He shifted from one foot to the other and back again.

"Think, Peter. I know a captain who will take you, but
if I put you under his authority you'll sail with the *Merry
Kate* to the east and be gone a long time. If you won't be
satisfied with less than the Royal Navy, you'd best say so
now, although you could very likely change over when
you're older."

Peter opened his mouth to insist, again, anything
would do, but closed it when his uncle raised a hand
warningly. Peter forced himself to think. He recalled his
father's stories. At the time they'd been exciting, but
now some bothered him—tales of floggings, of poor ra-
tions, and sea battles where whole ships disappeared
beneath the waves. Peter gulped. "Sir?"

"Yes, Peter?"

"What is the captain like?"

"He's stern but fair. His crew respect him and have
faith in him, but my friend is *not* a bosom beau to each
of his crew. He can't be. He's the captain. There is work
to be done, Peter, m'lad, and no one is mollycoddled."
Sec held up his hand when the boy started to interrupt.
"I know you don't dislike work, Peter. That is not the
problem. What you dislike is authority."

"I don't disli—"

Again, Secundus interrupted. "Then why do you
disobey your sister?"

Peter pouted. "Ruth's a woman."

"You have another excuse when it's Robert?" Secundus asked in that overly polite way which could hurt
deeply. Peter hung his head, and the toe of his shoe dug
into the dirt. "Are you aware, m'boy, you can be flogged
for disobeying your captain?"

Peter squared his shoulders. "I want to go to sea. I've

never wanted anything else. I know I've everything to learn, but I can do it. I *can*."

"Yes," said Secundus slowly. "Yes, I think you can. Have patience, Peter. The *Merry Kate* isn't due for weeks yet. When she arrives I'll have a word with Captain Horton." Peter's eyes widened and his face glowed. "There are conditions, whelp." Peter straightened. Secundus eyed the boy. "You'll attack your lessons with a will, and you'll obey your brother and sister."

"Yes, sir." Peter bowed. "Thank you, sir. I'd come to believe I'd never get to sea, you know, so nothing seemed to matter anymore," he confided. Peter was very nearly out of sight when he whooped with glee. The boy twirled and whirled and ran, jumping a hedge before disappearing.

Secundus stared after him for a moment before turning and coming face-to-face with Robert. Their eyes clashed. Secundus realized, belatedly, that perhaps he'd been a trifle high-handed. "Well, nephew?"

"*Can* you get him on a ship?"

"Yes. If you and Ruth don't forbid it."

All the younger man's antagonism faded away on an instant. "That's all right then. I feared you might be promising something you couldn't do. We never promise the children what we can't accomplish. It isn't fair."

"The boy will be at sea before the autumn storms."

Robert nodded. "It will be dangerous, won't it?"

"No more than if he were to go to London and get in with the wrong set—something he'd be bound to do once he was old enough, simply because there was nothing else for him to do." Secundus grinned. "I know."

Robert grinned, too. "Thank you, sir. I'll remember that when I need to soothe Ruth. She'll worry that he's wet or cold or falling overboard."

Secundus watched Robert return to supervising the work on the old barn. Thanks to Paulo, who had tactfully surveyed the Alcester property, Sec had a pretty fair notion of what was needed immediately and what might be put off.

So. The repairs were begun and he'd settled the problem of Peter. Just knowing he *would* get to sea had resulted in change. Immediately the boy was less sullen. Secundus wondered what else he must do. He should discuss it with his Helen. She'd know. In fact, why not? He brightened.

Half an hour later, Secundus walked around the outside of the house to the room where Helen had set up her office. He knocked softly on the French doors. No answer. Was he going to have to run the gauntlet of Maden and, possibly, her brother? Sec knocked again.

The door opened and his Helen stood scowling in the doorway, squinting out at him. "Yes?"

"Yes? Just yes? Well, since you agree. . . ." Sec put his hand at her waist, gently moving her inside as he followed. Almost before Helen knew for whom she'd reluctantly opened the door, he had bent to her, was kissing her. Awkwardly, her arms came up around his neck, and the kiss deepened. When he lifted his head, she lay her cheek against his chest, and for a long moment they stood silently. Sec sighed. "I shouldn't have done that." But his arms tightened around her.

"No. I shouldn't have responded." But she didn't move.

"Helen?"

"Yes, Sec?"

"I really shouldn't have."

"No."

"Because now, having had one, I don't think I can do without another."

"That's good."

Sec chuckled softly. He pushed her chin up and waited until she opened her eyes. Then he kissed her gently and let her go. "I'd like very much to seduce you, my love, but I don't think I'd better."

"No." She sighed. "It wouldn't be a very good idea, would it? Why *did* you come, then? If not to seduce me?"

"To ask advice. You said you'd help me settle my family. Well, I don't know what to do next."

"What have you done?"

He told her about his talk with Peter. "The lad was getting rather hot to hand because he'd lost hope. He'll do, now."

"When last I saw Peter he'd grown immensely. I wonder if he has anything suitable to wear to our party."

Sec rubbed his nose. "Hmmm. Clothes. He'll need kit for shipboard as well. And Robert. He's not quite reduced to smocks, but there's not much wear left in the coat he put on this morning. That's a good notion, Helen. I'll just take a little run into Lewes with the two of them. There must be a tailor of sorts there."

"He's a decent tailor, actually, but slow. You'll have to be stern with him, Sec."

"I'm very good at that," he said, and scowled fiercely, growling at the same time. She laughed and he grinned. "Well, perhaps not quite like that, but he'll have the necessary done in time, see if he doesn't. Thank you, love. That's just the sort of help I need. I'd not have thought of it."

"I'll think of other things, too." Helen tipped her head. "Sec, how would it be if I leave that door unlocked during the afternoon? You can come when you will, and if I'm not here you can ring for Maden, who will find me. What say you?"

"It isn't proper, Helen."

She grinned. "No it isn't, is it?" Then she moved into his arms for one last kiss before telling him he really must go now.

"I'll go."

She nodded. "Thing is, you'll be back, won't you?"

"Try if you can keep me away."

She didn't try.

In the next few days Sec made several visits to the little room at the side of the Hall. Seeing his Helen in private suited Sec right down to the ground. Seeing her in public was another thing altogether.

After the Sunday service Secundus stood in the churchyard. At this very instant, he thought, my Helen is only a few yards away . . . just inside the door. She's about to come out into the churchyard. I'll have to greet her as if I'd only just met her. Here where everyone will be watching. Secundus pulled at his limp cravat and an instant later found his forehead beaded with sweat. He wiped away the revealing moisture. But then he shivered, trepidation filling him as he anticipated certain disaster. He'd never been very good at doing the pretty. Treating his sweet little Helen as if he'd never held her, never kissed her . . . as if she were a near-stranger. He couldn't do it. He shivered again.

Instantly, Paulo, an expression of concern on his features, came forward. "Sec?" Secundus's head jerked around, his eyes staring. "Fever, Sec?"

Secundus grabbed at the excuse and babbled, "Yes. Yes, I think I may be coming down with a touch of the fever. Exactly right. You must get me home, Paulo. Immediately. Do tell the others you are taking me home." Secundus walked away, his step determined.

Paulo's concern changed to confusion. If Sec had already reached the stage where he was sweating and shivering, he should have no energy. Paulo had a quick word with Robert. Robert, finding it difficult to stop devouring his forbidden love with his eyes, also felt the need to escape an impossible situation. Lucy was held firmly to her father's side, and there would be no opportunity to talk with her—not that he would if there were. Rob hurried after Secundus and Paulo.

Ruth looked around for the young ones. "We must be off now," she said to them, but her eyes drifted to where Rotherford still spoke with the vicar. Their eyes met and Rotherford smiled. The baron excused himself to the vicar and approached. Ruth's pulse pounded erratically. Rotherford had not voluntarily approached her for years, unless one counted the day he'd come to see Robert. Suddenly, it seemed much less necessary they leave.

"Good morning. It was an excellent sermon, was it not?" he asked. His voice was bland, but his eyes were expressive, holding hers with a certain intensity.

"Very good, indeed," she managed. Shyly, she added, "Will you be so kind as to tell Miss Rotherford I'm looking forward to the call she kindly promised?" Duty fought with inclination and duty won. "I think my uncle is ill, he left in such a hurry, and feel I must get home to him. I've collected the children."

Once the Alcester party was out of sight, John joined the group where Helen was arguing vehemently in support of Miss Brown against Mr. Chalmers's views concerning the local workhouse. "The carriage has arrived," John inserted into a hint of a pause. "Gerry has been out quite long enough for his first step back into company . . . don't you agree?"

Helen gave her brother a look which told him exactly what she thought—which was that he used Gerry as an excuse to remove himself from the necessity of doing the pretty to their neighbors. However, Gerry did look a trifle down pin, so after one more unrewarded look for Secundus Alcester, she excused herself and they returned home for dinner.

* * *

Helen nodded to Maden once the second course had been served. The butler and the footman withdrew. "Well, John?"

"What is that in response to?"

"What did you th-th-think of the argument about the local workhouse?"

"I heard very little of it," said John, his expression unrevealing. He looked back down at his plate and paid careful attention to removing the bones from his fish.

"John, this is important. I spend my life doing what I can for those more needy than myself, and what do I find when I return but that I should have been working much closer to home!"

"Hmmm."

"John!"

"Helen," said Gerald, "he's teasing you. He talked my ear off not long ago about the changes he'll be instituting now he's the trustee, and you know very well he asked for your advice on such things."

"But," she said, "I didn't realize the problem was so urgent."

John looked up from his fish. "I'll not do it all at once."

Helen growled softly. "Why do you do it, John?"

"Tease you? Maybe because you take yourself so seriously."

"L-l-life is serious."

"You didn't used to be such a sobersides." It was Helen's turn to pay attention to her fish. "I remember how you once laughed easily. And often. You were something of a jokesmith," said John almost accusingly.

Gerald looked from one to the other. "I remember, too. You had a nice laugh, Helen." She glared at him. "*Have* a nice laugh?" he corrected himself in an innocent tone.

For a moment no one spoke. "Have I become such a b-b-bore?" she asked.

"Not a bore," said Gerry quickly.

"No, not that. Just . . ." John stopped, searching for words. "It's just that you've forgotten to laugh. I'd like to hear you laughing again."

"Sec could always make me laugh," said Helen softly.

"Could he? Then perhaps he was not so useless as I thought."

"Don't, John."

"He doesn't appear to be in any great hurry to see you again, does he?" Would she never admit she'd already had a meeting with the man?

"It would seem that way," Helen responded with no expression at all.

Had he come that once and not returned? John, suddenly worried about her lack of emotion, put aside his own feelings to ask, "Should I build a fire under him for you?"

"*John!* You wouldn't."

He chuckled. "No . . . unless you wished me to."

"Well, I don't." A sly grin lightened her features. "Besides, I'm not the least worried about Sec." She looked from one man to the other. "I know why he's not come."

"You do?"

"Yes. He hasn't found the bottom to face me," she said, lying with no compunction. This time her family was *not* going to interfere.

"Well I'd think not," exclaimed Gerry. "I'd not have the courage to look you in the eye after fifteen years."

"Maybe I *should* see about a fire," mused John, his eyes narrowing. What was Helen up to?

"You leave my Secundus alone. If any fires need lighting, I'll light them myself." She patted her mouth with her napkin, hiding a grin, and rose to her feet. "I'll be in my office. I've work to do—even if it is Sunday."

Gerald noted John's concern for his sister, clearly revealed now that she was no longer there to see. "You're worried. What is wrong, John?" he asked.

"I didn't think Alcester right for her fifteen years ago. Why would he be right for her now? Of course I'm worried."

"You didn't sound it when you were teasing Helen."

"I can't protect her if I'm on the wrong side of her, can I? You know there's no ordering Helen. One must lead her gently the way she should go."

"Except," chuckled Gerry, "very often, while you attempt to guide her, she sneaks off and does whatever it is, and has returned and is putting the halter back on before you've realized she's slipped it."

John grimaced. "Don't remind me. Gerry, I must discover what I can about Secundus Alcester. Fifteen years. Who knows what the man has gotten up to in fifteen years. I'll have to think how to go about it." He, too, excused himself, leaving by way of the French doors into the garden. It was time, thought Rotherford gritting his teeth, that he find out more about Secundus Alcester. It was a trifle deceitful to approach Miss Alcester with the intention of finding out what she knew, but that, he decided, was exactly what he was going to do. And why did he feel so good about such underhanded behavior? Just because it was an excuse to talk to Miss Alcester. He refused to think about it.

Gerry, left alone in the dining room, chose a pear from the centerpiece. He hoped Alcester hadn't gotten up to anything which would interfere with Helen's happiness. That is, assuming the man had an interest in her happiness. After all, so far there wasn't much indication Secundus Alcester had any interest in her at all.

Not that he knew of, anyway.

Six

"Frowning, Miss Alcester?"

Ruth sat back on her heels to look up at her unexpected visitor. Her immediate reaction was irritation that she'd been found in her present condition—hot, very likely covered in an unlady-like sweat, and her hair straggling from its knot—so she glared at Lord Rotherford's benign features. "Frowning?" she asked. "Me? Heavens no. This is my everyday dig-in-the-flower-bed face."

"What flower bed?"

His perplexed expression was so obviously that of a very bad actor that Ruth burst into laughter, forgetting to worry about how she looked.

"That's better. I like to see you laugh." The hint of a smile both in his eyes and the corners of his mouth disturbed her. He shook his head. "No, no, Miss Alcester. Not that frown again."

"Why are you teasing me?"

"Don't you like it?"

"I don't know."

Rotherford grinned at the unexpected response. Miss Alcester was forever responding in unexpected ways that kept him just slightly off-balance. He'd liked that when she was a girl. He found he still liked it. "I think I'll try it for a bit . . . until we know one way or the other?"

Since Ruth continued to kneel before the long-neglected flower bed, John dropped to the ground. He touched the leaf of a blue speedwell, clutched its stem, and pulled it. "You weren't frowning because of weeds."

"It isn't polite to call me a liar."

"Isn't it?" He watched her yank a buttercup. "Perhaps you should teach me my manners."

"I'm sure it's too late." He didn't reply in kind, simply looked at her with that warm interested look she'd known well when she was younger but hadn't seen in ever so long. She sighed, acquiescing to his silent request for information. "For one thing, I was thinking of Miss Chalmers."

"Our beloved squire came by the other day. He ate most of the seed cake after finishing off all the sandwiches Helen ordered up for our afternoon refreshment, but he wasn't the bluff cheerful man we know him to be." One dark eyebrow tipped up at the end, a querying look.

"You'd be unhappy, too, if you'd been spoiled to death and were suddenly bereft of pampering; if, normally, your every whim was catered to and all at once all at your home was ill-run and your meals a hodgepodge of whatever occurred to a cook always in need of strict supervision, and your daughter took you literally when told you didn't wish to see her face 'til she came to her senses."

John's eyes widened through Ruth's enumeration of Mr. Chalmers's problems, his expression more and more one of astonishment. "It isn't the least bit humorous, is it?" Ruth approved his reaction. "Why did she take him at his word?" he asked.

"To make him come to *his* senses, I believe." Ruth yanked a nettle and looked at the roots. "I don't think it'll work."

"How long has this been going on?"

"When I visited Lucy last week, the flowers were already dying in the vases. The sad thing is, given how stubborn they both are, it's likely to go on forever. Lucy isn't happy but believes it the only way."

"I'd ask Helen her views, but she's rather preoccupied by quite another visitor." Did Ruth know of her uncle's interest in his sister?

"Visitor?"

"You don't know, do you?"

"My lord, you speak in riddles."

"Do I? Then I'll speak plainly. Your uncle has come courting my sister. Again. What do you think of that?"

Ruth plopped back on the grass and hugged her knees, a slow smile widening her mouth. "He's courting Miss Rotherford *again*? Is that the story behind the story of why he went to India? We were told he'd suffered a wander-bug bite. He left quite abruptly, you know." Rotherford found himself curious. His interest encouraged Ruth to continue. "Father had sold out not long before—he was swept overboard on his last tour and nearly drowned, and, to be frank, I rather think he lost his nerve." Ruth bit her lip, wondering if she should have said that. But Rotherford merely nodded acceptance of the honor-blighting fact. "Uncle Sec came fairly often when we first moved here," she continued, "visiting Father's new property, you know. That last time he'd only just arrived when they had a monstrous row."

"So?"

"So Uncle Sec wanted a loan to get himself started, he said. Our father didn't object to the notion, but he'd put his fortune into the manor, here, and couldn't get his hands on any of the . . . the ready, I think he called it. He told Uncle Sec to wait a few months. Uncle wouldn't. I never saw him again until he came home a few days ago."

"Back about then Helen changed, too." It was Ruth's

turn for an encouraging look. "She was always more serious than Gerry or myself, but I'd thought it because she was older and female." Rotherford grimaced. "She's only three years my senior, but, at fifteen, three years can seem a century."

"I know," said Ruth with feeling. "Peter thinks me ancient."

He smiled. "In any case, she withdrew from the ton and not all our father's ranting and raving could get her back. She began her first orphanage with money inherited from her godmother."

"I've always thought Miss Rotherford a wonderful woman."

"Not many people give my sister a second glance when they discover her blue-stocking propensities, especially not then, when she was, to be frank, both overly plump and excessively shy."

"I think my uncle might have," said Ruth. "He's perceptive."

"I think he did." John frowned. "Damn . . . that is, drat it! I *know* he did." John's frown deepened, and he stared across the overly long grass toward the church spire. "Now he's renewed his suit. I wonder . . . hmm . . ." How did one go about asking if a woman's uncle were a pauper? This was more difficult than he'd thought.

Ruth tipped her head, plucking at the grass beside her and letting the blades drift in the breeze. "I don't know either well enough to say if a marriage between them would do," she offered shyly. "Miss Rotherford has always been kind to us and I'd love to have her as an aunt, but," Ruth shook her head, "I just don't know if they would be happy together."

Such innocence charmed John, but he needed to discover more about her uncle before he began to think in terms of "would-they-be-happy"! "May I be frank, Miss Alcester?"

"Of course."

"I fear your uncle may think to recoup his fortune by marrying hers."

Ruth's eyes widened. She laughed. "You don't know your sister very well, do you?" John looked puzzled. "It wouldn't be a bad union, I think."

"I'll not permit it if he expects to live off her inheritance!"

Ruth sobered. "Miss Rotherford would not allow herself to wed a fortune hunter—no matter if she loved him, she wouldn't do it. As her brother you should know how deeply serious she is about her charities. She'd never waste her substance on a scatter-good." Ruth paused. "However that may be, although my uncle hasn't shown signs of being a nabob, he can't be entirely pockets-to-let. He bought Robert a gelding and hired servants. He's paid for the materials Robert needs for repairs, and has ordered new coats for my brothers. He never cavils at anything necessary." A smile lit her face, set her eyes twinkling. "Since you've no way of knowing, I'd better explain that a very great deal has been found necessary."

"Then you think him—although not a nabob—able to support a wife?"

"A wife and nieces and nephews and what have you."

"You know that?" Rotherford eyed her expectantly.

His expression stopped her, her hand poised, full of just plucked grass. *This* was why he'd come—to discover what he could of her uncle's affairs. So. Shouldn't she be angry? She turned a glare his way, but reading the concern in his eyes, his fear for Helen's happiness, she couldn't blame him for doing what he could to protect his sister. But she didn't know anything. Not really. Not for certain. So why was she convinced her uncle hadn't come looking for a handout? He *might* be gulling them, spending what he had and eventually would ask something in return.

"You don't know, do you?"

"Know? I know what I feel to be the truth." She looked at him and shrugged. "I can't care if he's rich or not. If he spends what he has improving things here and then wishes to live off our little income the rest of his life . . . well, he's another pair of hands and willing to use them. We've more than enough room, and, besides, he has a knack for making us laugh. I think that last, all by itself, would be reason for keeping him."

John tipped his head. "You, too, believe laughter that important?"

"Because it is, isn't it? If one can laugh, one can bear most anything."

John was quiet, reminded of Gerry and the day he began laughing again. His next question caught Ruth on the blind side. "What were you bearing up under when I arrived? Other than Miss Chalmers?"

"Oh, dear. You had to remind me, didn't you? I'd managed to forget."

"Forget what?"

She glanced sideways, judging whether to admit him into her confidence. There was that special warmth again, that look she wanted to treasure. He held his hand out, palm up, in a gesture asking for trust. Trust? Rotherford? Oh, dear, should she? Not that he wasn't a gentleman, of course . . . and maybe he could help. It was so silly and she didn't want to bother Robert with what might be nothing at all, but she certainly didn't understand Peter these days. Maybe she didn't understand because she was a woman, and perhaps a man might be able to remember what it was like to be a boy and twelve years old?

He tipped his head to one side, his eyes encouraging. "Tell me?"

His expression warmed her, affected her breathing adversely. This wouldn't do. She must stop thinking of Rotherford that way! His coming indicated he might be willing to renew their old friendship, but that didn't mean . . . She drew in a deep breath and took the plunge. "It's mostly a need for information," she said quickly. "When you were twelve, did you change? A great deal?"

Rotherford, thinking back to when he'd first discovered the existence of the interesting differences between men and women, grinned.

Ruth flushed. "I don't think it's that." Realizing she'd revealed an understanding that, as a spinster, she ought not have, the blush deepened.

He grinned more widely, but only said, "No, very likely not. Not for another few years. How has he changed?"

Relieved he'd not taken advantage of that slip of her unruly tongue, she said, "Peter's intelligent, but he's lazy. Suddenly, I don't have to push him. About his lessons, I mean. He can't do enough. But most revealing of all, is that he hasn't been fishing for days," she finished with what she felt to be the clincher.

Rotherford cocked his head, curiosity a strong light in his gaze. "He's cramming? Why is that a worrying thing?"

"It's so very out of character."

Rotherford was silent for a moment, thinking. "Has it occurred to you the boy might be preparing for his future?"

"If only his godfather would make good his promise to get Peter a ship! Peter wants nothing else, you see."

"Ruth . . ." He gave her a sharp look, but she didn't seem to notice his quite improper use of her name.

Ruth merely ignored it. Now that she'd lost her shyness

of him, she found she enjoyed talking to Rotherford, but if he were to begin flirting with her, as the use of her name indicated he might, she must put herself on her guard. It occurred to her that that would be very painful indeed, that having finally conversed with the man as she'd not done in years, the stupid infatuation was already deepening into something else entirely. She was startled from her musing by the sound of Rotherford's voice.

"Isn't it possible your uncle had a talk with the boy? Alcester was gone a long time. It's a reasonable assumption he's developed connections and that he intends to find a place for Peter himself—and has told your brother so?"

Ruth chewed the notion over in her mind. "I don't see it. Why would such a promise set Peter to studying himself into a brain fever?"

At a half-perceived movement, Rotherford turned to the side. "Isn't that the lad now?" She didn't move. "Ruth, if you're concerned, then ask him."

She met his eyes, read encouragement, and got to her feet. "Peter." Ruth brushed off her skirt. "Peter. Come here a moment. Please?"

The boy turned off his route toward the house. He bowed politely to Rotherford before asking, "Ruth? I'm starving. Is it nearly time to eat?"

"You're always starving, and it is nowhere near time." Her brother's eyebrows drew together, giving the young face a worried expression. "Perhaps Mrs. Blough would give you a bun or a tart if you asked her nicely." He brightened and looked toward the house. To stop him, Ruth said, "Peter . . ."

"Yes, Ruth?" the lad asked absently. "Do you think treacle tarts?"

"Custard," she told him and ignored the fact that was her brother's least favorite. "Peter, could I ask you a question?"

Peter sighed, shifted his weight from one foot to the other. "Of course."

"Peter, why have you suddenly taken such an interest in your studies?"

"What?" He glanced at her. "Oh that. I want to be an officer, not a common seaman. May I go, please?" When she nodded he ran off.

Ruth stared after him, bewildered. "Did that make sense?"

"Yes, I think it did." Rotherford smiled at her. "It's not uncommon for a lad with his mind set on a certain future to think regular studies irrelevant. I'd imagine Peter discovered there is more to being an officer than knowing how to climb into the rigging and pointing a ship sou' by sou'east. Or whatever." He touched her hand gently, but said nothing when she carefully shifted away from him.

"It must have been Uncle Sec. I must remember to thank him—and you. I might never have found the courage to confront Peter if you'd not encouraged me. Thank you."

He nodded. "Now that you've lost that frown with which I was greeted, I may get down to the business of my call." He looked at her politely when she cast him an owlish look. Hadn't his business been to ask about her uncle? "I've my curricle and my bays," he said when she said nothing. "A pair of plodders, but I'm fond of them. Will you come for a drive?"

Drive with him? Ruth forced back a moment's panic. As usual, when undecided, she found aid in humor. She lifted her hands, the gloves she'd fortunately remembered to wear were quite dirty. Next she lifted her skirt—not enough to show her ankles, of course—and looked at it. Soberly, she faced the baron and blandly said, "I don't think so. Someone would see us and think you'd rescued me after an accident. It would be the newest *on-dit* in no time at all."

"If I offer to wait until you've changed?" he coaxed.

Ruth bit the inside of her lip. Her straightforward gaze caught and held his. "Why?"

"Why?" He blinked, slightly out of countenance at such a blunt question. "Because it's a glorious day?" he suggested. She shook her head. "The horses need the exercise?" She glanced at him, head to one side. "Because I enjoy your company?" he admitted softly. Ruth sighed. Dared she? After a moment he said, "It's wrong to enjoy your company?"

"I don't know." She raised worried eyes to meet his. "It depends."

Was Miss Alcester impertinent enough to actually wonder if he wished to set her up as his flirt? Or worse, his mistress? Even if the possibility had crossed his mind, he'd rejected the notion as impossible, hadn't he? How dare she? John's jaw tightened, a muscle jumping once. "I was raised a gentleman, Miss Alcester," he said. His gaze almost didn't touch her figure before it lifted to look over her shoulder and into the distance. Then, half admitting she wasn't altogether wrong, he breathed, "A fact I mustn't forget."

Ruth blinked. Surely he hadn't implied—no. He could not possibly have—good heavens, how could she have imagined such a thing?

"Run along, Miss Alcester. I mustn't keep my horses standing much longer." His eyes again said things her heart read even though her mind remained confused.

When Ruth went into the house, Rotherford strolled to where he could see his groom walking the team. He loved the way they moved, the sheen on their coats. A sense of peace enveloped him as he waited. It wasn't long before, somewhere inside, he heard her voice. He signaled for his rig and watched the groom, running at their heads, bring the team up at a trot.

Once they were on the road, Ruth spoke. "They don't look like plodders—not that I'm an expert, of course."

"I agree they aren't bone-setters, but then they aren't my blacks, you see." Ruth chuckled and settled herself. "Now," he said, "I suppose all you ladies are having pretty new gowns made for the party?"

"It's such an excellent excuse, is it not?" She explained in humorous detail about the blue silk and Lucy's gown. He asked about other things. She talked while he tooled along the lanes, chuckling often at something she said or the way she said it. She was still talking when he drove back up to the house an hour later. As he helped her down, she asked, "How did you do that?"

"Get you talking?" His left eyebrow quirked in the way it had. "How can one become acquainted with another if they don't talk?"

"Then you must do the talking next time, must you not, my friend?" Her eyes widened and color touched her skin. "Oh dear. That assumes there'll be a next time, and after prosing on as I did, that's a rash assumption indeed."

"If I'd been bored, Miss Alcester, you'd have been home long ago."

Ruth was bemusedly watching Rotherford drive off when Robert stepped up beside her. "That's a rather fancy suitor, Ruth. Climbing a little high, are you not?"

She'd have thought it an impertinent question if her brother weren't so obviously concerned for her. "I hope I know better," she said, the befuddlement dissipating. "But, on the other hand, given my advanced age, you'd think the man could find better things to do than to flirt with me." She walked off before Robert thought up a light response. Then, sequestered in her room, Ruth allowed herself to dream . . . a little . . . a little more than was wise, perhaps?

While Rotherford was discovering how much he enjoyed Ruth Alcester's company, Secundus Alcester was sitting in his sister's private room, watching her answer the last of the letters on her desk. "Have you finished?" he asked.

"Yes. I'm all caught up now," she said, turning in her chair, one elbow on the desk and the other on the chair back. "Have you been there long?"

"It seems forever. When you work, you put your whole mind to it, do you not?"

"It's the best way, isn't it? It is so easy to make mistakes."

"Yes. I wonder if I'm making a mistake with my family."

"How so?"

"Well, I'll help fix things up—Robert has the supplies he needs now for repairs—but then how does he keep it up? I don't really wish to give the children an allowance. I don't believe it good for character."

"If he had more land . . ."

Sec nodded. "I'd wondered about that. Who owns what Primus lost?"

Helen searched her mind and smiled. When she'd done explaining, Secundus smiled, too.

"Come here," he said, patting the other half of the small sofa on which he was seated. She looked a question. "So I can thank you," he said. "Properly." He leered a theatrical leer, his brows wiggling up and down. "And perhaps a trifle *improperly* as well?" She came.

Late the next morning Robert entered the house and called, "Ruth? Ruth! Where are you?"

She tripped hastily down the stairs and found herself picked up and swung round and round. "Robert! Put me down." He did, but held her with both hands. "Why are you grinning like a looby?" she scolded. "What has happened?"

"You'll never guess."

"Then tell me. Quickly."

"Remember when Tucker's boy died at Waterloo and the old man came here sick as a horse and asked if I'd like to buy back the big farm?"

"Yes. Poor old man. Losing one son to a bull that gored him and the other to French guns not six months later." Ruth shook her head. "No wonder he looked so bad."

"I had a talk with him a day or two later. He was feeling better and agreed to stay on until I could see my way clear to buying or to telling him for certain I could not. I'd about come to the conclusion I'd suggest he sell to Mr. Chalmers, who'd been nosing around."

"One would think our squire owned enough land," said Ruth, exasperated.

"I know. He's bought so much there's no common land left. And then he has the gall to complain life will be hard for the country people!" Robert shook his head. "However that may be, he won't get Tucker's land. We've got it!"

"How wonderful! Tucker will be happy to move into Lewes, I think. He'll be with his daughter and grandchildren there."

"Is that all you can think of, m'girl? What about us? What about looking the world in the face and paying our bills? Or knowing one can buy material for Peter's new shirt and still have sixpence for comfits now and again for Marie? Or," he looked her up and down and rolled his eyes upward, "some much needed lengths of material for new gowns for you, my dusty, dowdy, darling!"

Ruth ignored that. "Robert, how did we get it back? Tucker surely didn't give it to us."

Robert's shout of laughter brought Peter into the hall, ink dripping from his pen. "No, m'dear, he didn't give it to us. Uncle Sec did."

"Uncle Sec's doing us all proud, isn't he?" asked Peter.

"What has he offered you, you imp of Satan?" asked Ruth.

"A place on the *Merry Kate* when she next berths at London dock." Peter lifted the pen and stared at it. "I'd better get back to work."

Robert sobered. "I forgot to tell you about that, didn't I?"

"You knew?" she asked. Robert nodded. Ruth bit her lip. "Can he do that? Promise, I mean?"

"He seemed to think so. The *Merry Kate*. It sounds like a merchant's ship, Ruth. Do you think that's all right?"

"I prefer that to a naval vessel, if truth be told. Peter's less likely to find himself in the middle of a battle." Robert nodded and Ruth relaxed. She'd feared he'd want Peter to follow their father's footsteps.

Robert walked away, came back, started to speak, and walked off again. Finally he stopped and cleared his throat. "We won't be emigrating, Ruth."

"Moving? Oh, I'd forgotten that conversation."

"But if we're to stay here, I wonder—" He broke off, sighing.

"You wonder if Mr. Chalmers will find you a less objectionable suitor now that you've most of the land back." He nodded. "Rob, I just don't know. I don't wish to give you false hope." He shrugged, a morose expression belied by a certain fire in his eyes. "Rob, I'm sorry."

"Don't be, Ruth. I can't feel completely down when I've just been given back the biggest portion of what Father lost us."

"You don't feel guilty about Uncle Sec doing that for you?"

"No." Rob's grin returned in full, the twinkle back in eyes closely resembling his sister's. "I tried," he said ruefully. "I really did. He wouldn't let me."

"He has that knack, has he not? Of making you certain it's you doing him a favor when it's him just saving your life or something." She remembered Lord Rotherford's worries. "Rob, he wouldn't impoverish himself in order to help us, would he?"

"I don't think so. When he forked over his blunt, he didn't seem the least concerned."

"He's a generous man, Rob. We should offer him a home if he needs one."

"Or even if he wants one, which reminds me. He did ask about inviting an old friend down from London—Gubby, he called him." Rob grinned at her obvious distaste for the nickname. "More formally he's known as Sir Augustus Falconer, baronet. They were close friends before Uncle Sec left England."

"You told him it was all right, didn't you? That we've room for any guests he'd like to invite?"

"Yes. Then I tried to talk to him about Peter. He got red in the face and said he should have come to me before talking to the boy. He said it had been so long since he need consult with another, he'd gotten quite out of the way of it, and, besides, he'd forgotten I was officially Peter's guardian."

"I hoped you told him that we'll be forever grateful."

"I tried. He pooh-poohed any necessity to feel anything of the sort. He's our uncle, he said, and family, and anything he could do, it would make him feel better if we'd allow him to do it—the sort of line he feeds one when one tries to thank him." They looked at each other and sighed in concert. What their uncle forgot—or perhaps never knew—was that it was rather hard to feel like poor relations all the time, even when that was the truth of it.

"Well," said Robert, "I'd better see if Potts is setting out those seedlings under glass the way I prefer or the way he insists is right . . . not that I don't know what he's doing. He'll put in half one way and half the other, just to prove how wrong I am so I won't argue with him next time."

"Do you suppose he'll be right all down the line?"

"Of course he will. Just the other morning he informed me that I'm a mere pudden'head and don't know a wallflower from a cabbage seedling. There's nothing shy about our Potts. You won't catch *him* mincing words for fear of stepping out of line!" Robert stalked off amidst Ruth's chuckles.

"Well, Helen."

"Is it well, Sec?" She held out her hand.

"I don't know." He played with her fingers. "I think I've got the boys on the right road—thank you for telling me the Tucker farm was available, by the way—but I haven't a notion what to do about the girls."

"Ruth is what? Twenty-four? She's much too old to be treated like a child, Sec, but the little ones should be in the hands of a governess."

"The one called Tibby is a very interesting child, Helen. I won't have your average poverty-stricken lady who knows a bit of music, how to daub a watercolor, and is a dab hand at embroidery take that one under her wing. Do you know of anyone who would do, m'love?"

"I wish I did. My Brownie would be ideal, but she's retired."

"I don't suppose she's bored with retirement?" he asked, brows raised.

* * *

Helen's laugh belled out into the hall where John's head came up with a jerk. He'd just entered the house after a morning with his steward and was on his way up to change. Now he stood by the stairs, his hand on the newel and his nose very nearly quivering as he tried to hear what was going on in his sister's private room. Not that he could hear anything more than a murmur of voices, but Helen had *laughed*. It had been a long time since he'd heard her laugh so freely. He remained where he was.

"Bored? Brownie? Secundus, she doesn't yet know it, but, of course she's bored. It's a foregone conclusion she's bored." Helen chuckled again.

Sec looked like a hopeful puppy. "Don't suppose you'd come with me, reintroduce me? It's been a long time since we last met."

"I let you in here on the understanding you'd stay no more than fifteen minutes," she scolded. "I've those responses to sort"—she gestured to the bits of paper littering her desk—"and must check a myriad details. Dear Sec," she sighed, squeezing his hand, "I'll be so glad when this party is over and I may return to my own life."

Sec was silent for a moment. "Helen?"

She blinked. "Oh, my dear, you won't interfere. I think you'll rather enjoy my way of life, my heart." She held out her other hand, which he grasped firmly, looking down into her happy features. "Will you join me in my travels, Sec? Help me moan when I can't do more to help?"

"You know I'll support anything you wish to do, m'love."

Helen's laugh was softer this time. "I think you should discover exactly what that means before you make such a promise."

"I don't believe you could shock me, Helen."

"No, but I might run you ragged trying to keep track of me."

"You just try it." Sec squeezed her hands gently before raising one to his lips. "What would bore me is a woman I could lead by the nose." He turned her palm up, put another kiss there, holding her gaze as he did so.

Her laugh rang out again, clear and joyful. "Whatever else happens between us, Secundus Alcester," she scolded, gently retrieving her hand, "I can promise you, you'll never be bored."

Alcester's deep laugh rumbled into the hall, a bass counterpoint to Helen's lighter tones. John scowled. Since Ruth didn't know the man's financial situation, he must go to London to check into it . . . and he would just as soon as this dratted party was over. There must be someone—at the East India Company, perhaps—who could tell him something to the point. Not that it would do a bit of good to prove the down-at-heels miscreant was after Helen's fortune. Helen would only be angry with him for prying. Ruth was wrong that Helen wouldn't have the man if he were nothing but a fortune hunter, for the simple reason Helen wouldn't believe he could be.

Damnation. He couldn't sit back and do nothing. He wanted Helen happy. She'd been happy the past dozen years despite his halfhearted efforts to remind her occasionally of her position in Society—the annual garden party, only one instance of his maneuvering. She wouldn't be happy if Secundus took over her fortune and no longer allowed her to go on with her charities. What was a man to do? John's forehead creased deeply.

But then, once again, Helen's warm laughter wrapped around John, intruding on his thoughts. His scowl didn't lighten, but his mood did. Alcester brought out that lighter side in her and made Helen laugh. So maybe the man, fortune hunter or not, was good for her? That was almost as distressing as the notion the man could ruin her. But more than one charming vagabond had started by exhibiting an excess of charm to worm his way into a woman's affections, showing his true colors after the ceremony.

The door to Helen's room opened and Secundus backed out, hat in hand. He said, "You think I should go alone then?"

"If you want something done on the instant you'll have to."

"Just take an hour or two," he coaxed.

"I've not got a minute or two. She won't bite."

"If I come back covered with tooth marks, it'll be all your fault," jested Secundus. He closed the door on still another chuckle.

Helen's laughter very nearly made John waver in his determination. As a result, he was colder than he meant to be when he said, "Good morning."

Seven

Secundus carefully removed his hand from the door-knob to Helen's room. Now why, he wondered, hadn't he left, as he usually did, by way of the French doors? Sec wasn't ready to face Helen's brother. Not until he and Helen were entirely sure of each other. Well it was too bad, but these things happened. He turned, his eyes narrowing. What was going on in the bantling's head now? Not that John was still a boy. He wasn't. "Good morning," said Secundus cautiously.

Rotherford maintained a stern front. "You once promised me you were telling my sister goodbye."

"I did."

"I assumed you meant forever."

Alcester's eyes widened in pretended innocence. "Now where did you get such a crack-brained notion as that?"

John controlled a grin, drawn by the impudent suitor's expression. Was it any wonder Helen laughed more and seemed brighter and livelier? "It's obvious I erred," he said, dryly. "May I ask your intentions?" he asked politely.

Sec eyed Rotherford, who eyed him right back. The devil in Sec prompted him. "No, I don't think you may. Helen is a grown woman this time. She's under no one's authority but her own."

Take a Trip Back to the
Romantic Regency Era
of the Early 1800's

4 FREE BOOKS ARE YOURS!

4 FREE
Zebra Regency Romances!
(A $19.96 VALUE!)

Plus You'll Save Every Month With
Convenient Home Delivery!

We'd Like to Invite You to Subscribe to Zebra's Regency Romance Book Club and Send You 4 Free Books as Your Introduction! (Worth $19.96!)

If you're a Regency lover, imagine the joy of getting 4 FREE Zebra Regency Romances and then the chance to have these lovely stories delivered to your home each month at the lowest price available! Well, that's our offer to you and here's how you benefit by becoming a Regency Romance subscriber:

- *4 FREE Introductory Regency Romances are delivered to your doorstep (you only pay for shipping & handling)*

- *4 BRAND NEW Regencies are then delivered each month (usually before they're available in bookstores)*

- *Subscribers save almost $4.00 off the cover price every month*

- *You also receive a FREE monthly newsletter, which features author profiles, discounts, subscriber benefits, book previews and more*

- *There's no risks or obligations…in other words, you can cancel whenever you wish with no questions asked*

Join the thousands of readers who enjoy the savings and convenience offered to Regency Romance subscribers. After your initial introductory shipment, you'll receive 4 brand-new Zebra Regency Romances each month to examine for 10 days. Then, if you decide to keep the books, you pay the preferred subscriber's price, plus shipping and handling.

It's a no-lose proposition, so return the FREE BOOK CERTIFICATE today!

FREE BOOK CERTIFICATE

Treat yourself to 4 FREE Regency Romances!
A $19.96 VALUE... FREE!
No obligation to buy anything ever!

lll..l..llll....ll.l.l.l.ll..ll...l..ll.l..ll..l

REGENCY ROMANCE BOOK CLUB
Zebra Home Subscription Service, Inc.
P.O. Box 5214
Clifton NJ 07015-5214

"She's been there for a lot of years now."

Sec nodded. "Touché."

"Why have you come back?"

"I learned that, as a result of my brother's death, my niece and nephew needed me," responded Sec promptly.

There was truth behind that statement, and John recognized it. But there was a distressing corollary. "Do you mean you'd not have returned, even now, if it weren't for that?"

"Probably not." Sec shrugged. "One gets in a rut, you know. One thinks maybe next season—or next year— and the time comes and there's another something boiling on the fire or blowing in the wind and one puts off leaving yet again."

"Then your affection for my sister can't possibly be so very strong, can it?" This time John s voice was cold from anger.

Secundus threw an exasperated look Rotherford's way. "You're just full of idiotic observations today. If you'll think back, you'll recall that you yourself convinced me there was another, much more acceptable, suitor for Helen's hand. You told me in so many words your father had agreed to the match and that Helen would be married at the end of the Season. You were a very convincing young man, John Rotherford. I believed you," Secundus added, with a note of regret, his eyes full of pain.

A flush tinged Rotherford's cheeks. He'd forgotten much of what he'd said during the tirade he'd poured over the shabby genteel man who had changed his beloved sister all out of recognition. Now John could recognize he'd been jealous of the man his sister loved. Was he still jealous? Ridiculous.

"Well?" asked Sec sharply when he received no answer. "I should return to England to find Helen suffering in an unhappy marriage? Can you imagine the temptation to take her away from it? Do you think me so dishonorable?"

"I can only say that at the time I believed what I told you." For half a moment John dithered, then added, "But I'll admit that my belief was very likely based more in jealousy than fact."

Sec blinked. "Well now."

John's lips tightened. "But that doesn't mean you're any more proper a suitor for her now than you were then."

"Still jealous?" goaded Sec.

"Perhaps I am, but I believe it's that I've protected my sister from men who can't or won't understand her for a long time—men only interested in her fortune." Rotherford's jaw clenched, relaxed. "I'll have to see proof you aren't another of them before I stop worrying about you."

"I'll give her all the support she needs, if that's what worries you."

"Support her work? I'd rather you didn't. She's far too personally involved as it is and endangers her life every time she goes among the poor. Her health, of course— the wretched have always been carriers of disease—but it's more. In the current unsettled economic climate, violence is a very real possibility. The Luddites in the north are only one instance."

Secundus rubbed his nose. "I see I need to know a great deal more about what's going on in England than I've yet had a chance to learn. It wouldn't do for rabble-rousing weavers to pop her over the head with a sley, would it now?"

"Joke if you must, but the weavers *are* up in arms. They and others. She puts herself into danger whenever she goes off on one of those study tours, as she calls them."

Sec grimaced. "What makes you think I'm joking? Why

can't you admit I love your sister? She has something I've found in no other—a *mind*, which you'll admit is a rarity among women in this addlepated modern world. Another thing you've never admitted, Rotherford, is the importance of laughter, but she and I have always known and know we make each other laugh. There is enough to trouble one in everyday life. Laughter is the only decent way to survive it."

John barely heard anything after the first words. "Love." His lips tightened and relaxed. "I presume such an emotion exists, although I've no proof of it. That makes it very difficult to trust someone's, anyone's, profession of love."

"You love your sister."

Rotherford shook his head. "That isn't what I mean."

"Love is a many-sided thing, boy. You could deduce the one sort from the other if you weren't such a stiff-necked, fish-eyed, stubborn, nose-to-the-sky twiddlepoop." Sec eyed his unwilling host warily. "Sorry. Lost my temper. But that you love her should hint to you about other kinds of love."

"You really don't know when to shut up, do you?"

"Never did," said Sec and shrugged.

Much to his disgust, John again found humor in his outrageous guest's attitude, and a bark of laughter escaped him. "For Helen's sake, you'd better leave. If we come to blows, she'd get into it, and we neither want that."

"Very true. So, I'm off to see Miss Brown. Does she bite?"

"Bite?"

Secundus sighed. "I need a governess for my young nieces. Have you ever interviewed a governess?"

"No. Of course not."

"I'm shaking in my boots."

"Careful they don't shake apart at the seams," said

John, and then immediately regretted such ungentlemanly behavior. He'd not forgive someone for saying
such a thing, so what could he expect from the man facing him? John squared his shoulders and waited stoically
for justified anger.

It didn't come. "They've seen more than I like to remember," said Secundus, bending, fists on his hips, to
look at the items in question. "They should be given
honorable retirement, but unfortunately this is the only
pair to my name that isn't falling apart! Ah well. Maybe
they'll hold. I wish Helen would go with me," he finished
plaintively. "I've faced a regiment on the verge of rebel-
lion and a tiger with wet powder. I've lived through fever
and plague and diseases too numerous to name but—
except for my Helen—I've never liked facing women.
Every man has his fears."

"Why don't you take your eldest niece. Surely she'd be
the one to decide the question in any case."

Secundus brightened. "Ruth. Now why didn't I think
of her? Not that it's a question of deciding. It's finding a
way to convince Miss Brown she wishes to take the young
ladies—one of whom will never have two thoughts to rub
together and the other one who can't seem to crowd in
enough notions to fill her up. Thanks for suggesting I
take Ruth. Excellent notion, that."

John watched Secundus out the door. Could love exist
between such an odd pair? His beloved sister, with her
dowdy little figure and her occasional stutter? A tall gangling man, with thinning hair, who dressed at random,
choosing from items with never a jot of style and poor
quality to begin with? The romantic poets would have a
good laugh at such a pair.

Love. John shook away the vision he couldn't get out
of his head of Ruth holding her youngest sister, the two
of them nose to nose and grinning happily at each other.

He'd observed them in the village, just that way, several weeks ago and why he couldn't forget that scene bothered him. It had tempted him to indulge a whim and renew his old acquaintance with Ruth. Then, using the need to know more about Secundus Alcester as an excuse, he had gone to see her and ended the visit by taking her for a drive.

She'd been delightfully natural; she'd asked his advice about the boy, Peter. And her prattle later when driving— none of the flirtatious nonsense he found off-putting in the Society misses in London. They discussed nothing unsuitable or a trifle warm, but Ruth had a knack of twisting a conversation in odd and delightful ways. He looked forward to talking to her again, which was all very well, but he must take care. He was not ready for marriage. When he was, he'd choose carefully, as he'd planned, from among women trained for the position he'd be offering. Having made that very sensible decision, he went back to daydreaming about Ruth Alcester—an occupation which proved most enjoyable if rather time consuming.

While John thought thoughts he knew he really shouldn't think, Secundus stood beside his team, undecided as to what to do. It was unusual for him to dither. Finally, he told the Rotherford groom to hold them just a bit longer and turned back toward the house, but not to the front door through which he'd just come. Instead he strolled around the side and along the path there. When he reached Helen's study, he took a moment to watch her working away industriously as she had when he first arrived. But when she put down her pen and shifted back in her chair and seemed to stare off into space, he tapped at the window, turning the door handle at the same time. "Helen?"

She turned, a hand to her breast. "Secundus Alcester! What a start you gave me!"

"I'm sorry. I just can't seem to go away. I tried, you know. I got so far as taking the reins from the groom holding my team. But I couldn't manage to step up into the carriage." He shook his head mournfully. "Terrible thing when a man can't even get into his own carriage," he added.

Helen chuckled. "You are cutting a wheedle." He nodded several times, rapidly, firmly. She grinned. "Well?"

"Come?" he asked. "We'll take Ruth who, as your occasionally quite intelligent brother pointed out, should have a hand in it and we'll all go see your Brownie. You see," he said, putting on a wide-eyed innocent look, "I still can't quite manage to get over the notion she bites." He held out his hand.

Although his mouth was spouting nonsense, his eyes were saying quite other things. It was too bad, thought Helen, that she could only guess at what. She remembered just this sort of thing from when he'd first known her and he wished her to do something he knew she didn't really want to do. If she said no, he'd go away. It would never again be mentioned. There would be no recriminations, no pouting.

On the other hand, he never asked if he didn't truly wish her company. Very often he had hidden his deepest feelings under a clownish mask. She thought it was true again, now. She looked down at the desk. Except for a few items of charity business—which she'd already set aside for later consideration—there was nothing which needed her attention. Sending him away earlier had been an exercise in control, both of him and herself! Because she wanted to be with him so badly, knew he, too, wished to spend more time with her—because of that, she had refused him.

"Helen? Is it so difficult to say a simple yes or no?"

"But it isn't simple, is it?"

Sec put his mind to that conundrum. "You mean you fear you'll set a precedent of always giving in to my wishes?"

"It isn't even so simple as that. I don't wish to give into my wishes so easily either." She sighed. "Don't you see, Sec? It is tempting to abdicate my duty and forget every other important thing and for no other reason than to spend time with you."

"Have you a duty you must attend to just now this instant?"

"Well . . ." She hesitated. "No."

"Then?"

"Then it is perfectly all right to come with you. Especially since you need protection against Brownie-bites." She grinned. "One moment, Sec, while I get my bonnet and have a word with Maden. You wait right here now."

Curled up in an unlady-like fashion in her window seat, Ruth stared toward the pasture. Uncle Sec's pair were gone. Briefly Ruth wondered where, but the question slipped from her mind at the thought of other horses. There was Rotherford's team of so-called plodders, for instance. And long ago, there'd been a half-broken two-year-old, black as a moonless night. Ruth plumped her chin down on her knees. Why had she been so foolish, when still a girl, to lose her heart to a young god on a stallion? Well hidden, she'd watched the young John Rotherford schooling the animal. Instinctively, she'd known the gentle firmness he displayed was a side he rarely, if ever, showed the world.

Ruth sighed. It was all very well to nurse a hopeless passion, but it was quite ridiculous to allow it to interfere in the business of life. This daydreaming, for instance. So wasteful of time and energy. Why couldn't she allow herself to be courted by . . . Lieutenant Ralston, for instance? He wasn't wealthy, but was known to enjoy an easy competence. He could care for her and the girls and, thinking of his friendship with Tibby, she thought he'd be pleased to do so. So why not?

Ruth's glance turned from the bright day to roam her room and was caught by the high old-fashioned bed, the steps essential for climbing into it set neatly beside it. Her cheeks warmed and she buried her face in her skirt. She knew very well why she wouldn't encourage the Lieutenant. She couldn't, wouldn't—her head snapped up, the knock on her door interrupting thoughts she was glad to have disrupted. "Yes? Come in."

"Mr. Alcester says, begging your pardon miss, but could you give him a moment of your time, miss?"

Ruth looked out and saw the carriage.

"Oh, miss, Miss Rotherford as well, if it please you, miss.

"Tell them I'm coming, Mary." Ruth flicked her skirts in the hopes she'd rid them of some wrinkles. A brush smoothed back the wisps which insisted upon curling around her face, and quick fingers firmed the pins which kept her long tresses wound up. She grimaced at her mirror, wishing she were more up to the knocker, as Peter would say. One more flick at her skirts and she left her room.

"Miss Brown?" asked Ruth once Secundus had explained. "Yes, of course she'd be good for the girls. But she's retired now."

"So Helen says." Sec smiled at Miss Rotherford. "But, the woman I recall will be bored to tears. Have you ever met a woman with a wider knowledge of our world? Or better able to transfer that knowledge to young heads?"

"She'd be ideal . . . for Tibby especially."

Niece and uncle looked at each other. Unacknowledged was the fact that Tibby seemed to have her share of intelligence and that of her sister Marie as well. Ruth sighed, and the sound was echoed by her uncle. They smiled a trifle wanly.

He cleared his throat. "What I want, Ruth, is that you come with us when we talk to her. She might be willing to come out of retirement for someone as special as Tibby, don't you think?"

"Maybe," suggested Ruth, only half in jest, "you should take Tibby."

"Brownie will long ago have made a judgment about both girls," said Helen. "She'll know." The smile she exchanged with Ruth was full of understanding and was followed by Sec's unmistakable look of approval.

"But your brother pays her a pension, does he not? Why should she consider taking on another pair of young misses?"

Sec said, "Some don't do well in retirement. I'm thinking Miss Brown is one such."

Ruth sincerely hoped he was correct. "I'll just find my bonnet."

During the short drive to the other end of the village, they marshaled every possible argument to convince Miss Brown. None were needed. "Be governess to that young Tibby?" asked Miss Brown partway through their first tentative presentation. "I thought you'd never ask." Miss Brown, it was decided, would start lessons after the garden party.

After returning Miss Rotherford to the Hall, and once again on their way home, Ruth said, "I was surprised at how warmly Miss Brown greeted you, Uncle Sec. How is it that you know her so well?"

"Knew Miss Rotherford before I went to India." Sec's neck reddened. "Was courting her, you see." Ruth nodded. "You know the story, do you?"

"No. Only bits and pieces. More guesses than fact."

"We fell in love," he said with great simplicity as he pulled the team to a walk. "We thought we were special, of course—that no one had ever felt as we did. Silly of us." He shook his head. "But Miss Brown approved our relationship. Think she must have been the only one who did, unless maybe Maden did. Rotherford's butler, y'know."

"You mean Helen's family thought you wrong for her?"

Sec chuckled. "Unprincipled fortune hunter was the mildest epithet young John threw at my head when he discovered I'd the audacity to look to his sister. Very protective bantam, the lad was. Admired his spirit even when I wished him to the devil. I knew I wasn't a fortune hunter—loved my Helen, you see, and didn't even think of her fortune—but, even so, I knew I wasn't a proper suitor for Miss Helen Rotherford's hand."

"So you went to India to make your fortune?"

"I went," he responded dryly, "because I was told in words quite unmistakable that a marriage had been arranged for my Helen. If I'd stayed in England I'd have eloped with her. Couldn't have helped myself. But, eloping's no good for a woman." Secundus sighed. "I deliberately cut myself off from word from home, fearing I'd hear how unhappy she was. If I'd known she was free, I'd have come back years ago." He chuckled and his eyes twinkled wickedly. "Oh, nine or ten, at least."

"Which means," mused Ruth, "you'd have stayed away five or six. Which means what?"

"Which means," Sec admitted, his grin a trifle lopsided, "that India and I got on like a house afire. We fit," he finished with a shrug. He dropped his hands, and the team picked up its pace. Wondering what she'd read into that statement, he tossed a sideways glance toward Ruth.

Ruth, accepting that the conversation was finished, didn't read much of anything into it. She turned her thoughts to the guest who was coming. "Will you tell me about your friend?"

"Gubby? You'll like old Gubby. He'll not trouble you," said Sec with the ignorance of someone who never had to worry about company. "I asked him to oversee the delivery of some supplies I've ordered—hurrying them along, you know."

"You've asked Sir Augustus Falconer to . . . ?" Ruth thought of the finicky ways of the few tonish men she'd met. The mind boggled at the notion of any of those languid men actually overseeing tradesmen. "Uncle Sec," she scolded, "you can't have done anything so *outre* as to ask a tulip of the ton to act your agent."

Sec, biting his lip, looked at her, looked back at the road. She giggled. He rubbed his nose and a chuckle escaped him. "By Old Nick's noggin, that's just what I've done, isn't it now! Gubby will have a word or two to say on the subject." He threw back his head and roared with laughter.

"Poor man," said Ruth when he stopped.

"Poor man if he doesn't. Gubby likes his food. And wine. Good wine."

Ruth flushed. "And our cellars are bare."

"Don't hand me a Cheltenham tragedy, niece. It's no fault in you the place fell on hard times. My brother was a fool of the first order. He should have known he'd no head for gambling."

Ruth held her tongue for a long moment, then speaking with a certain diffidence, she ventured, "I don't think Father ever felt quite the same after he fell overboard that time."

"You mean he lost his nerve and then had to prove to

himself he wasn't a coward? Bah. Not only a coward, but witless as well."

"Uncle Sec . . ."

"You wish me to cease speaking ill of the dead? Well, I will. I'll not speak of him at all." He changed the subject as they turned in the Alcester lane. "Hope Gubby remembers to bring my new boots and coats. I'd like to make a proper show at the garden party, don't you know?"

"If Peter's to go, his new coat better be finished as well. He's outgrown the old."

"The tailor in Lewes will have the boy's clothes ready in good time. I was told he's slow, so I put a flea in his ear." At Ruth's questioning look, Secundus added, with an odd simplicity which implied it was, or should be, obvious, "Told him we wouldn't accept the order if it weren't done in time." He hopped down from the seat. "It's easy to get service, Ruth, if one knows the way of it. The man was insolent. I let it be known we'd go to Brighton for what your brothers require if he got on the wrong side of me."

"Brothers? Require?" Ruth bit her lip. "Uncle Sec, did you order clothes for Robert, too?"

"Of course. The lad's wardrobe is in very nearly a worse state than mine, which is saying something, is it not? Besides, he's added muscle since his last coat was made. What's more, both of them need more than one decent pair of proper trousers. Then, I've been told there will be a deal of entertaining once Rotherford's do is over. Robert will need evening gear."

"Oh dear, we're such an expense to you."

"Hmmm. Didn't think, did I? You'll be needing new clothes, too." He rubbed his nose again, eyeing her speculatively. "Maybe we'll take a little run up to London for your wardrobe. That's what we'll do. We'll stay at a nice hotel and you can order just what you need."

"What I need? A wardrobe . . . for me?" Ruth remembered how nice it had felt to don Lucy's pretty dress. But should she allow . . . ? "Oh dear."

"Come now. You aren't the blushing sort, m'dear. You've been far too practical these past few years. Had to, o'course, but it's time you had a few pretties. We'll find us the very best modiste. I'm determined you'll shine among the other young women."

"I'll confer a great boon on you if I agree?"

"That's the way of it, of course. Paulo," he added as the man approached, "we'll be going back out immediately." He gestured at the horses. "They'll want a drink, but don't unhitch them." Secundus took the shallow steps to the open door almost at a leap and disappeared inside.

Ruth frowned. "Tell me, Paulo, why does my uncle dislike being thanked?"

"What has he done now?"

"Offered me a new wardrobe made up in London by a tonish modiste."

"The money means nothing. He gets pleasure doing things for his kin, and the pleasure means a great deal."

"But shouldn't we worry about the cost?"

"He'll not outrun the woodworker." Paulo frowned. "That doesn't sound quite correct."

"Outrun the carpenter," she said absently. "Paulo . . ."

"I'll not discuss Sec's business," he said, a warning note in his voice.

Sec came back out of the house in very nearly as much a rush as he'd entered it. "Not watered them yet?"

"No. Not yet."

Secundus gave his friend a sharp look. "Been saying things I don't want said?"

"No. Not that either."

The men grinned at each other.

Ruth looked from one to the other. "You are like a pair of little boys with secrets."

The grins widened. "Exactly," said Secundus, his tone one of utter satisfaction.

A little later, as he and Paulo took the turn toward Brighton, Paulo asked, "Where are we off to, most excellent second son?"

"We're visiting an orphanage, Paulo."

"Orphanage? That is a special place for children?"

"Yes."

"Why are we visiting this place for children?"

"Why? Because I wish to see what sort of place my Helen supports."

"Your Helen pays for it, oversees it?"

Sec glanced at his frowning friend and chuckled. "What do you really wish to ask, you Polly Pry, you?"

Paulo frowned. "Paulo Pry? What is this Paulo Pry?"

"*Polly* Pry, my curious friend. It is someone who snoops in another's business. Now what is it you wished to know?"

"If we do not like the orphanage, will it make a difference to us?"

"Of course not—not in any way which counts." Secundus's voice dropped to a confiding tone. "Thing is, I'm a trifle worried about how I might help Helen—how I can contribute. I'll have a better notion of what part I'll play in her work once I've seen how one of her charities operates."

"Won't your fortune play a role?"

"Money! Anyone can give my Helen money. I wish to do something."

"Do something?"

"Yes. We won't have much of a marriage if we can't work together, will we? And, after waiting all these years,

Paulo," said Alcester softly, "I want to do all I can to make it the most beautiful life possible."

"Am I to give you congratulations, honored friend?"

Secundus's ears burned. "Well, yes and no. Nothing formal is decided between us. But soon, I think. But not just yet, anyway. Well, not at all if I don't find the courage to approach my Helen. Properly, I mean. Just sort of hinted, you know, now and again."

Paulo smiled at his friend's babbling. "I understand."

"You do?" Sec looked surprised, then rueful. "Wish I did."

"But it is simple. You fear she will say ye nay."

"That's clear enough. Except she's been doing some hinting, too, I think. What isn't clear to me is why I've become so spineless."

"You will find your courage and roar with the roar of a hunting tiger, oh second son of much honored Alcester."

Diverted, Sec said, "You know, Paulo, if you'd ever come face-to-face with that Alcester you honor so much, you might not feel so favorably toward him."

Paulo's brows rose. "But I thought you knew. My reason for revering honorable senior Alcester is that he produced a son such as you."

Sec blinked. Was Paulo serious? Or not? Perhaps better not to ask.

"I have another question, honored son of honored Alcester."

"Let me hear it."

"Would it perhaps be more tactful if you were to come to yon orphanage with your Miss Helen to guide you around it?"

"Tactful?" Secundus drew the team to a halt. He stared down the road toward the roof of the stone-built house, which one could just glimpse among old trees. If he'd not been misdirected, it was his destination. He was, perhaps, a quarter mile from its gate. Helen was nearly six miles back the way he'd come. Yet, didn't Paulo have a point? Wouldn't Helen enjoy showing him her achievement? "By Old Nick's knee-britches, this learning to think as if two were one isn't easy is it?"

"Am I to understand that you agree with me?"

"Yes, blast you, I do. Don't you think you might have made your point before we got quite so far from home?" He stared down the road. "So, it seems I should ask her to come with me. On the other hand I haven't a notion when she'll have time to give me a tour."

"Is it that she, too, has much to learn about this business of thinking as if two were one?"

Secundus chuckled. "We've both been thinking for ourselves for a long time now. Do you think either of us can learn the trick of it?"

"You, Secundus Alcester, can do anything you set your mind to doing."

Sec's ears burned. "You needn't upset the butter bowl."

"The butter bowl? Why would I wish to do something so foolish as upset a bowl of butter?"

"Butter me up. Flatter me."

"Ah. More of this strange English where the words mean other than their meaning taken one by one."

"It's called cant, Paulo. The language is rich in it. Some of it is acceptable before the ladies, but most isn't. Take care how you use it."

"I see. I shall be very careful indeed about using this new way of speaking." One of the horses twitched his ears. The other shook his head. "Have we," asked Paulo politely, "decided whether we go on or go back?"

Sec set the team in motion. "We go back. It's occurred to me that going without my Helen might be thought to be going behind her back."

"That would be bad. Especially if it were our Helen who thought it?"

"Exactly. So. We'll come another day. I think I can turn here, don't you?" he asked as they came to a slightly wider place in the road.

"You look sad, my genie," said Tibby, plopping down beside Gerry. She touched him gently when he didn't respond. "Should I go away?"

"Tactful child. No. Don't go. I just don't feel like talking."

"Then I'll be quiet." She plucked daisies, and when she formed a crown she lay it on his hair, continuing her work in silence until he touched the new chain questioningly. "This one's for me. See?" She tossed it over her head and arranged it against her faded blue dress. "I'm on holiday until after the garden party," she added, Gerry having indicated he'd no longer object to conversation. She reached for a daisy, plucked the petals off one by one. "Then Miss Brown is to be our governess. Do you know Miss Brown?"

"Yes, I know her." He watched idly for a moment. "Why the frown, Tibby? Don't you want a governess?"

"I'll be all right," she said stoutly. "But Marie . . . Marie . . ."

"Marie worries?" Tibby nodded, still frowning. "I know Miss Brown rather well, child. Do you want me to warn her about Marie?"

"Would you?" She gave him a worried look. "Miss Brown won't get cross and scold when Marie can't do things, and shout, maybe?" The line that permanently creased Tibby's forehead deepened still more. "Marie gets very sad when she can't do things. She cries."

"I'll explain that to Miss Brown, too, if you like."

Tibby sat, hands folded in her lap and stared at Gerry for a long moment. "You're a very special genie, did you know that?"

"I'm not a genie at all." For the first time that day his Tibby smiled. That surprised Gerry, for his tone had been sharper than he'd meant it to be. "I thought we'd settled that."

"Of course you aren't a genie . . . except to me." She grinned an impish grin and said, "You won't forget, will you, that you owe me yet another wish?" He batted at her playfully, and she ducked the reprimanding hand. "I've been thinking," she said, "that it would be a very good thing if you wait until I'm all grown up big enough and then you marry me."

He started to grin, saw she was serious, and swallowed a laugh. "Tibby, I'm fifteen years your senior," he said gently. "By the time you're old enough to marry, I'll be very nearly an old man. Like Rotherford," he said to clinch it in her young eyes.

"Pooh. Rotherford is the perfect age to marry." Gerry didn't ask whom she'd overheard indulging in that bit of gossip. To clinch her argument, she added, "Besides, you'd still be my genie, my special friend."

Gerry sighed. "You are too young to understand, but believe me, Tibby, one needs more than friendship before getting married."

Tibby nodded. "Like Mary and her young man. Mary walks out with Mr. Chalmers's groom. They hold hands and kiss." She looked up, mischievously. "Mary is our maid, you see. I followed her on her day out."

Gerald stared. "Child, do you really think it permissible to spy on people? It isn't," he continued before she could answer.

"But I don't have any other way to find out things."

Gerald drew in a deep breath. "Listen to me, Tibby. That sort of thing is wrong. You mustn't do it anymore."

"I won't have to, will I? I'll have Miss Brown."

Gerry thought of the maid and kissing and who knew what else. "Some things shouldn't be explained to an eight-year-old. You don't understand."

"That's what Ruth says when I ask hard questions. 'You're too young, Tibby. Someday you'll understand.' But it takes so long for someday to come, my genie. I can't wait."

"When I speak to Miss Brown about your sister, I think I'll discuss some other things, too. You, my girl, need a hand where it'll do some good if you think you should have everything you want right now."

Tibby frowned. "But I *don't* think that. I can't marry you until I'm at least sixteen. Ruth says it's not proper before then. That's a very long time."

Gerald hovered between irritation and laughter. "Minx! You can't just decide to marry me even if you do manage to reach adulthood without someone doing you an injury. You have to wait to be asked." She shook her head. "Young ladies don't do the asking." She pouted. It was a look Gerry had never seen on her face. "Tibby, you may turn a man down, once he's asked, if you don't wish to marry him, but you can't go asking him to marry you."

"But that's silly, isn't it?" The unusual touch of petulance faded. "Don't you see? The right man might not know a lady wishes him to ask."

"Why don't I ask Miss Brown to explain such things to you? I know that that's the way of it. I don't know the *why*." Tibby turned that over in what Gerald believed to be an exceedingly precocious mind. For a moment he thought he'd managed to sidestep the issue neatly. He was quickly disillusioned.

"I see," said his imp. "It's another of those silly rules made up to make life com-pli-cated beyond belief." She sighed, a ridiculously adult sigh. "When I grow up I'll ignore the rules—oh, only if they're silly, of course, like not asking a man to marry you."

"Tibby, believe me, your life will be far more complicated if you don't live by the rules." He'd definitely have to have that talk with Miss Brown.

"Well, then, when I'm old enough, will you ask me?" she asked on a wistful note.

"You don't understand."

She sighed again, a combination of exasperation and something very like despair. "People are always telling me that."

"Has it occurred to you, m'child, that's because it's true?"

She frowned. "You mean," she said slowly, "that there are such a lot of things I don't know about and it's too much to tell me all at once. But because I don't know about them, they make what I do think I know wrong because what I think I know doesn't think about those things."

Gerald drew in a sharp breath. "That was a trifle hard to follow, little one, but if I sorted it out all the way through, yes, that's exactly why you don't understand."

"I'll grow up and know all that. Then I'll understand."

Gerry blinked. "Tibby, I hate to admit this"—he touched her curls lightly—"but I don't think anyone ever understands everything."

"No, of course not," she responded immediately. Then she popped in another flush hit. "Only God knows everything. Like the vicar said last Sunday. God is om-nis-something. It's a long word which means," she explained kindly, "that He knows everything. But one can know as much as one is able to know, can't one?"

Poor child. To have that mind and to be a girl. "Tibby,

I'll talk to Miss Brown. I don't know the sort of things you need to know." When she opened her mouth, he added, "Miss Brown will know how to find out if there is an answer to be had." Gerry could say that with confidence.

His imp stared at him for a moment and then nodded, seemingly satisfied. Again they were quiet while Tibby collected more daisies. "It is a very complicated world, is it not, my genie?" she said after a long silence.

"Very complicated indeed." Not wanting another discussion he wasn't certain how to handle, he changed the subject. "Is that daisy chain for me?"

"If you'd like." She finished it and threw it over Gerry's head. "If I make another would you take it to Miss Rotherford?"

"I will." Gerry smiled. "She'll like hers as much as I like mine."

Gerry took Helen a neatly made daisy chain. He also gave her the wreath he'd forgotten he wore until Maden's stare reminded him, the butler unable to keep his eyes away from it. Helen wore the slightly wilted flowers to dinner.

"You are setting a new fashion, perhaps?" asked her brother.

"Not at all. I am merely being appreciative of the thoughtfulness of someone I like."

John looked at Gerry. "Did that make sense?" He took a second look, stared at the flowers lying against Gerry's chest. "It is a new fashion?"

Gerry laughed. "No, only a gift from someone rather special."

John felt a tightening in his chest. Special. He lifted his wine to his mouth to hide his feelings. Whom would Gerry honor by wearing so silly a thing as a chain of daisies? Ruth? Gerry and Ruth? The notion was not, for reasons he preferred not to consider, a happy one.

Eight

"Well, Secundus?"

"Not well. Not well at all." Secundus grasped the hand Helen held out in sympathy. "I've erred," he said with a great deal of earnestness. "Helen, I don't quite know how I came to forget something so simple, but I did. Now what do I do?"

"If I knew what it was you were talking about . . . ," said Helen, hiding a smile even as she wondered what could have rattled Secundus so badly.

Sec straightened. "Eh?" He blinked rapidly half a dozen times. "By Old Nick's nappy, haven't I said?"

"Secundus, all you've told me is that you've erred." She chuckled. "I can see why you're in a dither, of course. It must have been the first time in your life you've done such a thing."

He didn't laugh as she'd expected, but changed the subject. "No. Not the first time. That was when I believed that pup of a brother of yours, and the second was when, knowing the pain I'd feel upon hearing you were un-happy, I cut myself off from news from home." His hand tightened on hers. "Helen, how could I have been so stupid? The years we've wasted."

"Not stupid, Sec. Just desperate and hurting, as I was, here at home. But," she added, gently prying at his hard grip, "we both made good lives. We have nothing of which we need be ashamed."

His hand relaxed and absently soothed where he'd squeezed. "I don't know that I've done nothing wrong, Helen. In fact, there was that time I . . ."

This time Helen's hand tightened around his. What sort of women had he known in India? Had they been beautiful?

Sec shook his head. "But you aren't interested in old business matters where I was perhaps just a teensy bit underhanded when in competition for some prize. No, what I need to talk about is Ruth. I didn't *think*, Helen."

Only business? How dare he frighten her so? "About what, Sec?"

"About clothes, Helen. Why, I doubt if she's had a new dress in even longer than you've had one. I gave her that silk, you know, and thought I'd taken care of the immediate problem, but I forgot you can't go hiring dressmakers if you haven't a penny piece to your name. Why didn't I think to hand over housekeeping money? Now it's too late, what with the party coming up so soon and all. I erred, don't you see? How can I fix it, Helen?"

Helen relaxed. "You can stop worrying. Ruth has managed very well."

"She has?" He relaxed when Helen nodded. "But how?"

"She took the silk to Miss Chalmers who has a reputation for cutting dresses. There's a trick to it, you know." When Sec denied he knew any such thing, she laughed. "In any case, young Lucy thought silk too precious for a mere garden party and, since she will not attend, made over her dress for Ruth."

"Well, now. Lucy Chalmers, you say? Don't think I know the child."

"Not a child, Sec. In fact, I think you'll find she's

infatuated with your nephew, and, if I'm not mistaken, he returns the feeling."

"I hadn't a notion the boy was courting someone."

"He isn't. Mr. Chalmers doesn't approve."

Sec scowled. "He doesn't?" His lips pressed into a firm line. "Well, now, we can't have that, can we?"

Helen smiled. "I think we should give Lucy a chance to see if her present scheme succeeds before you step in to make things right."

"You'll tell me if I should do something?" Helen nodded. "So that brings us back to Ruth's wardrobe. Helen, I promised her a London modiste, but I'd rather forgotten about things like chaperons. You see, we've no choice but to stay at a hotel, and I may be her uncle, but I'm a stranger to the ton and they may not believe it. Will you come with us? To make things right."

"Oh." Helen put her finger to her chin. She pursed her lips and then, after a moment, shook her head. "It is quite embarrassing, but I can't think of a soul I know well enough I could write and ask if you and Ruth might stay with them for a week or two. All my friends go to the country for the summer. Perhaps John is not quite so wrong as I'd thought," she finished, her forehead creasing.

"John? What has that interfering pup been saying to you now?"

"It's nothing to do with you. He merely suggested that I spend too much of my time out of the ton." She shook her head. "If, amongst all those from whom I solicit money each year, I can't call even *one* my friend, then he has a point."

Sec tipped his head. "Helen, m'love, that gives me a notion." Sec pulled her closer and hugged her. "I just happen to know someone who lives almost entirely in the ton. He'll arrive any day now." Helen's brows rose. "Hadn't I told you? I've invited my old friend Gubby Falconer for a visit. You remember Gubby? He'll know just how to go about it, including which modiste to see." Drawing her along with him, he strolled toward the French doors through which he'd arrived. "So, now that's settled, I think I'll kidnap you," he said with a perfectly straight face.

"You jester." She smiled up at him from the circle of his arm.

Half a second later the smile faded as, after opening the French doors to the garden, Secundus picked her up and carried her out. He rounded the house to where the landau waited and, setting her in, climbed in behind her. Paulo gave the team the office and they were off.

Helen sputtered.

Secundus laughed.

"Stop at once!"

"No. I need you."

Helen eyed him, glanced toward Paulo's back. Color climbed her neck and into her face. "Secundus Alcester, have you lost your mind?" she hissed.

Realizing she'd misunderstood him, Secundus's easy laugh turned to a roar. "No, no," he said, wiping his eyes. "It isn't that." He glanced sideways and, finding she was glaring at him, he winked, "Although it *is*, of course, in another way, but," he sobered, "what I'm needing just this instant is a guide. You, my love, are to show me around that orphanage of yours and tell me all about it."

"My orphanage? Today? But, Sec . . ."

He took her hands and raised first one and then the other to his lips. "Love, is there truly something you must do this hour? Because, if there is, we'll turn and go straight back. Or is it that you've arranged your life to such a tight schedule, you've no time left in it for me?"

"Oh, Sec." The former flush faded. Her skin paled still more, and, her eyes worried, she gazed up into his. "Is that how it seems to you?"

"A bit. Because, you see, I'm a bit that way, too. It worries me. Have we gotten so set in our ways, Helen, we can't alter?"

Helen thought about it, staring into his eyes. She squeezed his hands and smiled. "You know, there isn't a thing I can't put off to later. And I think the most delightful thing I could do today is show you my orphans. They are such good children, Sec. You'll adore them just as I do, m'love. And if you'd seen where some of them came from, you'd wonder at all they can do. Why, you just wait."

"Really Lucy, you've done far more work than you should have." Ruth held up the gown, amazed by the sprays of satin-stitched flowers embroidered on the skirt.

"One tires of memorizing poetry, you know."

Ruth mused, "I've wondered if Robert's changed circumstances might be in your favor." Ruth explained about Uncle Sec buying back the farm. "So you see we are no longer quite so poor."

"Hmmm."

"Do you think you'll go to the party after all?" teased Ruth.

"I've sent my regrets, Ruth. Besides, Father hasn't quite understood how firm I am. I'll not marry at all if I can't marry Robert."

"He won't throw you out?" When Lucy tipped her head, questioningly, Ruth asked the more bluntly phrased question, "He won't disinherit you?"

"Oh, no . . . unfortunately." Lucy grinned at Ruth's shocked expression. "Then Robert would marry me, to save me from a life of servitude, you see."

"Your father's a good man, Lucy."

"Of course he is. But stubborn. He knows Robert

would make me a wonderful husband and that Robert would make him a fine agent. He just can't bring himself to let me go to a poor man. But if Robert has the farm back . . ." Lucy moved to the window, then turned back. "That's for the future. Put the dress on, please, Ruth. Let's see if I need do anything more to it."

"I'd say all that embroidery was doing a great deal already," said Ruth, trying to lighten her friend's mood.

"I mean to the fit, silly." A few minutes later Lucy stood back, and a smile of satisfaction lit her face. "Just wait, Ruth Alcester, until Rotherford gets a glimpse of you in this."

Ruth blushed all the way up into her hairline. "You mustn't say such things, Lucy. Even if your dress impresses him, nothing can come of it."

Later, when Ruth came down the stairs, Mr. Chalmers stomped out of the front parlor where he was talking to a visitor. He left its door open, in his rush to intercept her.

"Good morning," said Ruth a trifle overbrightly. Carrying away the dress meant for his daughter gave her a guilty feeling.

"Miss Alcester." He bowed. Ruth waited for him to go on, but after clearing his throat twice, he managed only, "Well, well."

"Did you wish something, Mr. Chalmers?"

He hemmed and hawed. Finally, "M'daughter. Is she well?"

"Lucy appears to be in good spirits."

"Good spirits." He rose on his toes and settled back. "Humph. Doesn't mind at all not seeing her old father?"

"I think," said Ruth kindly, "that she minds very much, but isn't allowing that fact to defeat her. She can't oblige you, you see."

"Humph." His hands went behind his back where,

Ruth guessed, he was clasping them tightly. "Humph." He raised up on his toes and rocked back. "Well, then." He searched for words but ended by blurting, plaintively, "Don't understand the chit. Don't she know I only want the best for her?"

"Mr. Chalmers, should you say that to me? Robert is the best." She held up her hand. "Not in a worldly way, of course, but he's willingly shouldered his responsibilities, never wavered in caring for me and the little ones, has he? Nor did he go behind your back when you made clear your objections to his courtship. Keeping his distance hasn't been easy for him."

"Humph," he said, gruff again. "Don't suppose your uncle came back a rich man, did he? Know he don't dress like it, but it seems to me he's been throwing around the possibles pretty freely."

Ruth stiffened. Was everyone interested in her uncle's finances? "That's none of my business." Her tone grew colder. "I've not asked and I won't. I can only be thankful for the aid he's given us."

Mr. Chalmers's skin darkened at what was clearly a reprimand. He cleared his throat again before he managed, "See why you're scolding me, Miss Alcester, but I need to know if your uncle means to do right by the boy."

Ruth's features hardened and her tone cooled still more. "If he'll inherit from a nabob, then you'll take him? Mr. Chalmers, that isn't worthy of you. A man's character is far more important than how wealthy he is."

"No, it isn't." His chin squared stubbornly. "Marriage is an arrangement. It's all very well if it's happy—most often it's well enough—but marriage must take account of land and money. Of future generations."

"Why?" pounced Ruth, suddenly seeing her way.

Mr. Chalmers's eyes bugged. "But it's obvious."

"No it isn't," she insisted. "Explain it to me."

Behind them, Rotherford appeared in the parlor doorway. Originally he'd been upset at being placed in a position where he'd inadvertently become an eavesdropper. Then he'd become interested.

Mr. Chalmers hemmed and hawed. "It's always been that way."

"You mentioned future generations," Ruth said, feeling a trifle guilty for guiding his thinking. "Do you mean so they'll be happy?"

"Of course." For an instant Mr. Chalmers relaxed.

"But why shouldn't the last generation's marriage make this generation happy, instead of this generation making the next one happy?" Ruth hid her glee at having the chance to voice her conclusion.

Mr. Chalmers's mouth opened. Slowly he closed it. He stared at Ruth. Then he looked up the stairs. When he turned back, it took a moment for him to focus on Ruth's face. "Miss Alcester, there's a flaw in your argument. I'm certain there's a flaw, even if I don't see it just at once. I must think on it." He bowed with absentminded gallantry. "Good day to you, Miss Alcester. Let me show you out."

Rotherford moved forward and cleared his throat to announce his presence. Ruth, turning, flushed rosily. He smiled at her. "Mr. Chalmers, I think I, too, must be leaving. I'll think over what you've said, of course. Miss Alcester? May I escort you home?"

Mr. Chalmers watched them go. He wasn't happy Rotherford had gone. He wasn't certain he'd quite convinced his lordship of all he'd wished to say. Once he'd thought over Miss Brown's arguments concerning the workhouse, he'd decided she wasn't altogether in the wrong. When he'd met Rotherford in the road earlier, he'd invited him to step in to discuss the situation. After all, if a decision were made to alter the rules, then *Rother-ford*, as trustee, would be responsible, and it would be unnecessary for Mr. Chalmers to admit he'd ever been in the wrong! But it had seemed that Lord Rotherford had had his mind on some triviality or other, and one couldn't be certain one's words had had proper effect.

The triviality interfering so much with Rotherford's concentration on the important matter of the work-house was Ruth Alcester, whose laughter, mingled with Lucy's, had floated down into the hall just as Rotherford entered the Chalmers house. Then, just now, her notion that a person's happiness might be important—enough so, one might set aside social imperatives demanding quite other behavior—was a new and tempting thought.

Somehow, when he wasn't paying attention, it seemed his future happiness had become tangled with that of an unsuitable—from a rigidly conventional point of view— woman. But, there was nothing innately objectionable in Ruth Alcester as the wife of a baron. Why should she be blamed for the actions of her father? So why shouldn't he, Rotherford, think seriously of asking Ruth to marry?

Marriage? The notion sent cold chills down Rother-ford's spine. Then he remembered an odd dream he'd had recently in which Ruth looked up at him, a veil over her hair, a dim background populated by, he knew with-out knowing quite how, all his friends and relatives. It had been a surprisingly satisfying dream, but when had he begun to dream of marrying her? What had become of the old, exceedingly familiar, dream in which he walked toward his bed and found her there awaiting him, her eyes heavy with passion? That dream he could understand. But marriage? The shiver was less intense this time. Hmmm. Marriage.

"You are very quiet, my lord," said Ruth when she could stand it no longer. Why, if he wished to ride in a brown study, paying her no attention—let alone distinguishing attentions—had he offered to escort her?

"Huh? Oh, I'm very sorry, Miss Alcester. I was thinking, you see."

"I did see. Might one be impertinent and ask the obvious question?"

"You mean, what was it which had my mind a hundred miles away?" She nodded, a dimple flirting at the corner of her mouth. He grinned, his eyes twinkling. "Perhaps someday, Miss Alcester, I'll tell you what I was thinking. But, at the moment? No. You may not be so impertinent."

"That's set me in my place has it not?"

"Has it? Somehow I doubt that very much." Before she could respond with a suitably light comment, he turned the conversation to more serious matters. "It is true, then, that your brother and Miss Chalmers wish to be wed?"

She glanced at him. He rode along steadily, staring straight ahead. "I thought the whole world knew of their blighted love," she said dryly.

"I rarely listen to gossip," he said, apologetically. "I wouldn't have listened today, but the door was open and your voices carried to me clearly. I admire you for your loyalty to your brother. You argued well in his favor," he said stiffly.

Ruth felt the teeniest twinge of irritation. It wasn't what Lord Rotherford said, but *how* he said it—that air of condescension. "Thank you," she said in a crisp tone.

Rotherford glanced at her. Why were her lips so tightly pressed together? What was she trying not to say? Because quite obviously, there was something. "Have I said something wrong?"

"Not a thing, my lord."

He blinked. "Miss Alcester, would you do me the favor of being honest with me?"

She glanced his way. This time he was staring down at her with an intensity which could only mean she had his full attention. She swallowed. What should she do? Then she shrugged. If he wanted the truth, he'd get it. "It was not what you said, my lord, but the way you said it, as if you were surprised I could argue rationally, or that I could feel something so idealistic as loyalty."

"I certainly didn't feel either of those things. If I was stiff or rude, it was because I am unused to giving compliments to young ladies."

"For fear they'll get the wrong idea concerning your intentions, my lord?" she asked, the hurt deepening. "You needn't be afraid of me." It was Ruth's turn to stare ahead. Desperately she wished old Sugar weren't as slow as treacle in cold weather. If only she could remove herself from this embarrassing conversation.

"It is true," he said dryly, "that I would be unhappy if a woman took my words in a fashion which would lead to her suffering any unhappiness, but my dear Miss Alcester, my problem is that I don't know how I wish you to take them! Good day," he added, tipping his hat and, before she could respond to such provocative words, he turned down a lane and disappeared.

Since the lane led onto the downs, petering out into nothing, his taking it could only mean he was desperate to part company with her. Ruth stared after him for as long as she could without leaning around the edge of the rig, saddened that somehow, in only moments, they'd come to cuffs.

How had it happened? She went back over their words one by one. Yes. It had been her fault. She should not have been so honest with him, even if he had requested it. But wasn't their friendship worth nothing if it were impossible to speak one's mind? She sighed. Perhaps the problem was that there was no friendship, that she'd only imagined he had an interest in her. The pain in her chest, the need to find a solitary place and cry, became so great she, too, turned up one of the many trails into the uplands, though she didn't go too far. She was quite herself again when, sometime later and once again on the way home, she met the lieutenant and stopped.

"Has Miss Rotherford done her usual wonderful job of organizing the garden party?" she asked after the usual greetings were over.

"John is thinking of an innovation this year. He's toying with the notion of putting up a tent with a dance floor and hiring musicians. If he does so, will you save me a waltz?"

The pleasure she'd experienced at the idea of an alfresco dance faded rapidly. "Waltz? But I don't know how." Ruth pokered up. "One of Lucy's aunt's letters spoke of it. Lady Morton's sensibilities are outraged."

"Does that mean one must, on principle, disapprove?"

"One hears such stories, Lieutenant." She tipped her head and her cheeks grew rosy again. "Perhaps it would not be out of the way to mention that in a letter from her cousin Lucy was told a different tale. The youngest Miss Morton is enthusiastic. Every young lady she knows is learning the steps."

"On the Continent the dance is popular. As more officers sell out and return to Society, you'll find they insist the waltz become acceptable in every ballroom. It is delightful and, truly, although it can turn into a sad romp, done properly, there need be nothing even suggestive about it. I wonder if John would hold a morning waltzing party."

Ruth bit her lip. Oh, to be invited to such an informal party where she'd perhaps be taught the waltz by Lord Rotherford. She imagined his hand at her waist and her hand in his as Lady Morton had written was the way of it. She closed her eyes and shuddered.

"Miss Alcester?"

Her eyes snapped open.

"Are you all right?"

"I've decided I don't approve the waltz," she blurted.

He chuckled. "Lady Morton convinced you?"

"I do not take Lady Morton as a model and it isn't kind to tease me. I was thinking and I believe I understand why it isn't approved." Her color fluctuated from an interesting paleness to high color and back again. She met the understanding in his eyes and immediately looked away.

"You've been imagining yourself waltzing, haven't you?"

"Yes." This was another revealing admission, and she blushed hotly.

"Please withhold judgment until you've actually seen the dance done as it should be done," he coaxed, ignoring her reddened cheeks.

"Of course. Not that I'll have that opportunity any time soon."

Gerry smiled. "Don't be too certain, Miss Alcester."

She glanced at him. "The waltzing party? Even if Rotherford agreed to something so daring, you'd have difficulty finding people who would care to attend."

"You'd stay away?"

"Yes." She closed her lips on a desire to say of course I'd come.

"In that case there is no reason to suggest such a thing."

Her eyes flew to his, and he smiled. Again the expression was a warming one. Ruth didn't know how to answer so looked away and said nothing.

Gerry decided Ruth was far too easy to bait and not a young woman who understood flirting. She was of an age she should have become bored with the game of hearts, but it seemed no one had even begun to teach it to her. Such slow-tops the young men round and about must be. In any case, it was time to leave her before he succumbed to temptation and went too far. "I must be going, Miss Alcester. I'll see you again soon. Good day to you."

Ruth clucked, and the cob lifted its head and then one foot and then another and reluctantly began plodding along the lane home. As they neared the manor and Sugar's stable, the old dear lifted his feet just a trifle more quickly. Ruth reminded herself to order him a nice handful of oats as a treat.

After giving the new groom instructions concerning Sugar, Ruth took the dress to her room. Lucy's dress was, by far, the loveliest thing she'd had to wear in years. Would Rotherford like it? She thought of their misunderstanding and firmly put all thought of him from her mind. She'd shed enough tears about that.

And, the lieutenant? Had he been teasing her or flirting with her? And if flirting, why? She wasn't the sort with whom men flirted. Rotherford had made that abundantly clear. The moment she grew to womanhood, his lordship had ceased to treat her as anything more than a rather awkward acquaintance, unlike those years when she been a great gawky colt of a girl and he'd teased her and joked with her. Those had been happy years. Why, she wondered, had he changed so drastically? If it had begun just after her father's suicide she might have understood it, but it was before their ruination had become public knowledge. Since she had no new ideas on a subject she'd often debated with herself, she hung up the dress and turned her mind to the botheration of trying to think of something with which she could occupy her time!

Something other than daydreaming about their noble neighbor, that is.

* * *

Later that afternoon Tibby joined Gerry by the pond as was their habit.

"Hello, my imp," he said.

"Hello, my genie." She slipped her little hand into his. "Lord Rotherford took Ruth for a drive the other day. It's nice Ruth had a treat."

Gerry seated the child with adult courtesy and hid a smile at Tibby's graceful acceptance of his aid. "Having servants isn't a treat for her?"

Tibby's head tipped in that thinking way it had. "Ruth says she doesn't know what to do with herself and must find ways to keep ock-u-pied. Now that we're to have a governess, that's something else she won't have to do— teach me French and the globes and mathematics so I can keep accounts. Poor Ruth."

"What about music and embroidery and Italian?" he asked solemnly.

"Italyun?"

"I understand it is a necessary part of a young lady's education."

"That's all right then." Tibby leaned against his shoulder. "I don't think I am a young lady, so it doesn't matter, does it?"

Gerald frowned in earnest. "What do you mean by that?"

"Young ladies," she said slowly, trying to put into words just what she *did* mean, "have dowries and grow up to have a Season in London with pretty clothes and they are presented to the Queen and then they marry rich men with titles and give them sons and then . . ." She shook her head. "I don't know what they do then because I was told to go away and play. I'm always told to go away and play."

Gerald hid his relief his imp was basing her belief on nothing more than another overheard conversation. "It's good to have a dowry, Tibby, but not all ladies do. Nor do they all marry a title. Some marry plain misters."

"Oh." She mused a bit. "Well, it doesn't make any difference does it?"

"It doesn't?"

"No, because I've already decided." A grin lit her suntouched features and she flashed a mischievous look his way. "*You* are to wait 'til I grow up so I can marry you, 'member?"

"I thought you understood the problem with that lovely idea. I can't stop getting older while you try to catch up. You'll find someone right for you when you get old enough." Gerry smiled and squeezed her hand.

Tibby didn't look convinced but said no more on the subject. Instead she asked, in a repressive way, if he'd really suggested that Ruth learn to waltz.

When Gerry stopped laughing, he admitted he had, and they had a rather interesting discussion about dancing in general and the waltz in particular. Gerry was relieved Tibby didn't return the conversation to her future. He liked his little imp a great deal, but his mind was wandering toward the delights of much older imps, ones who knew what a man had in mind when he paid them a certain sort of attention. He also thought, now and then, of the more polite amusement of flirting with tonish young ladies at balls and soirees, so long as one were careful to make clear one was merely flirting, of course.

"Well, Secundus?" Helen asked when they'd started home.

"Very well indeed. I'm impressed." He glanced around,

saw no one was in sight—except the back of Paulo's head—and popped a quick kiss on her cheek.

"Did you think I'd have anything to do with an operation which wasn't up to snuff?" she asked, her cheeks rosy.

"Don't scold, my love. I knew very well you'd do things properly. Do you check up on the running of the place regularly?"

"More often than I'm able to do with some of my projects, Sec. They are so scattered and I don't get to all of them as often as I'd like."

"Perhaps in this I may help you. Helen, I won't be giving up my business. Will it bother you if I'm considered a cit?"

"You know it won't. Rotherford may cavil, but I won't let that bother me. Is it important, Sec?"

"I fear business will take me over the countryside a trifle more often than I'll like, you see. But, when I'm on my necessary travels, I can perhaps look in on any of your projects which are nearby?"

Helen looked at him and found him staring at her with a hopeful look. 'Would you *like* to do that, Sec?"

He took her hands. "I couldn't think what I could do, but this is one thing, I think. Helen?" Tears glistened on her cheek. He caught a drop, brought it to his mouth. "My love," he said urgently, "what is it?"

"Oh Sec. Sec," she chuckled, a rather watery sound, "it's so strange to have someone truly interested in what I do." She cradled his hand to her cheek. "I've been so alone, Sec."

He drew her gently into his arms. "Never again, m'love," he said, his voice choked. Staring over her head, he repeated, "Never, never, again."

Nine

The door to Helen's sanctuary burst open only to be slammed shut. "Helen Rotherford, is what I've been hearing true?" His fists pressed to his hips in angry knots, John scowled down at his sister's unresponsive head, which remained bent over her work. "Helen!"

"I suppose it depends on what you've heard." She continued writing with firm strokes of the pen.

"Look at me, Helen. This is important."

"When you come bursting into my private room, knowing I'm busy, and demanding my attention, I'm to docilely stop and listen to you rant and rave?"

"It is not I who is in the wrong, and what is more you are well aware of it or you wouldn't be behaving in this stubborn manner."

Very carefully, Helen placed a full stop at the end of a sentence. She set the pen in the inkwell. Then slowly she turned to lean one elbow on the desk and the other on the back of her chair. She watched John pace angrily around the small room. For a moment she let him pace, but when he stopped to look at her, she asked, "Now, what is this nonsense you are howling about?"

"Nonsense! It is nonsense that you go haring off with that man and nary a chaperon in sight?"

"Ah. Now I wonder who has been telling tales." He glowered. "But it was all quite convenable, John. I rode nowhere in a closed carriage with anyone, which is what you must have heard to be making such a cake of yourself." Thinking about what had happened—not that being held gently in a warm, loving embrace was all that much—she smiled slightly. Putting the memory away, she asked, "Now, what is the problem?"

"You were going along the Brighton road."

Ah. Not the journey home.

"Helen, you *know*—"

"We visited the orphanage," she interrupted.

His mouth open, he stared. Then, more quietly, "The orphanage?"

"Sec wished to see one of my projects in detail."

"Couldn't you have taken Miss Alcester along for propriety?"

"I suppose we could. Neither of us thought of it. John, it isn't as if I were seventeen and he a rogue." She watched him for a few more moments. "Is that your only objection?"

"You know it is not." He took the few steps to the windows and back, a frown creasing his brow. "You know I don't trust the man." His scowl softened, and his eyes begged her to understand. "I fear for your future if it becomes entangled with his."

"John, I am four and *thirty* years old."

"Helen, you are my sister," he said, mimicking her tone, his manner joking but his eyes serious.

She chuckled. "Will you allow that I do very well organizing and running my charities? All of them? That I don't become flustered when faced with a complicated situation? That I understand how to use money and how my fortune is invested and that I watch any changes made in those investments?"

"Helen . . ."

"I am not a child, John. I will not hand my capital to a

fortune hunter and allow my projects to die. And, leaving aside the money, I often think I am better fitted to understand other people and deal with my emotions than you are with yours."

A wary look crossed John's face. "Well, if you say it was an open carriage. . . ."

"Running away, John? It's all right to berate me about mistakes you think I make, but I may not tell you that your hermitlike existence is wrong? You interfere in my life, but I may not object to yours?"

"Oh, well, if you think I should get out and about more."

"John, why are you so unwilling to spend time among your peers?"

A grimace of distaste crossed John's face. "You truly don't wish to know. Besides, it is but a mishmash of little things. The women's shrill affected laughter; unmarried women's inane and flirtatious ways; deep doings at the club—too often by those who can least afford it." He shrugged. "Things I don't like and have ceased, therefore, to have to do with them." She continued to stare at him. "Helen, I come to London spring and fall to see my tailor and bootmaker. I check, then, with our solicitor so he need not come down here as he does, if needed, the rest of the year. I attend a few parties and see a few friends." He shrugged. "What more do you want of me?"

"Find a wife," said Helen promptly. "You've turned thirty. You don't live the sporting life as do so many of your contemporaries and you've no desire to travel. You love your estate and spend a deal of time caring for it. Surely you wish a son to whom you may leave it." She watched his growing unease. "Get you a wife, brother mine.

John stared out into the garden. "It has crossed my mind."

"Any w-w-woman in particular?" asked Helen, her tone

verging on the bright social voice she adopted when embarrassed. When wishing to turn John's thoughts from her future, it hadn't occurred to her she'd do more than irritate him. Now she wondered where the conversation might be headed. He didn't respond, just stared. "John?" she asked, worried now. He turned, seemingly undecided. "Can I help? Have I been b-b-blind? Is it that you've fallen in love with someone who is t-t-tied to another?"

"Nothing like that. I just can't quite make up my mind whether . . ." He hesitated, opened his mouth to speak, but closed it. Finally, he said, "Helen, when I decide to wed, you'll be among the very first to know." He walked to the door. Exiting, he closed it softly behind him. Helen was still staring at it when he stuck his head back in. "Sneaky Helen. Just like when we were in the nursery. Will you someday explain to me how it is that when it is you who are at fault, we somehow manage to end up discussing my faults?"

He ducked back out before she could do more than open her eyes wide. Helen turned back to her work, chuckling softly. He was right, of course, although it had taken him a very long time to see it. She'd always used the ploy, and quite successfully, too. Helen raised her pen, her eyes focused on the picture hanging behind her desk. It had occurred to her he was less likely to be tricked by such maneuvers in future. She'd have to think up something else! Helen bent to her writing, only to look up with an impish grin a moment or two later. The next time John complained *about* Secundus, she'd send him to complain *to* Secundus. That would fix him.

The day of the party dawned with that odd summer haze which told the weather-wise it would grow bright and warm. Lucy, realizing it at an early hour, also realized she'd forgotten to give Ruth the parasol which went with the dress. She rang for her maid. With the connivance of various servants, Lucy was soon mounted on her favorite hack and jogging along the lanes to the Alcesters'. She arrived just as Robert exited the front door.

"Lucy!" A flustered look crossed Rob's face. "Miss Chalmers, I mean."

She smiled down at him. "You meant no such thing, did you, Robert?" It was the first time he'd used her name to her face and she reveled in it, although using that as an excuse to say his was pure self-indulgence. "Now help me down, please. I must take this to Ruth and return home immediately."

He automatically reached for her waist, set her on her feet, but couldn't bring himself to let her go. "Lucy . . ."

"I know. I know, Robert." They stared at each other for a long moment.

Peter appeared in the impetuous manner of his youth and slammed to a halt. He came down the steps to the drive in a more gentlemanly fashion and bowed. "Miss Chalmers? Are you going with us to the party?"

Lucy forced her gaze from her love's, irritated by the interruption to a rare moment when Robert allowed himself to admit his affection for her. She took a second look. "Peter. Why, how smart you are. A regular tulip."

The boy blushed, a red tide rolling up his neck and into his ears. "No such thing!"

"Quite right," Lucy said with the seriousness the situation demanded. "A tulip would demand more in the way of dash when it came to waistcoats, would he not?" Peter still scowled. "But I shouldn't tease you. You look very well, Peter."

Robert took mercy on his brother's embarrassment. "You came to see Ruth, Miss Chalmers? Shall I send up to her?"

"She's in her room? I'll join her there." Lucy wasn't ten minutes with Ruth—just long enough to give a bit of advice about her hair—before tripping down the stairs into the hall. There, instead of Robert whom she'd hoped to see again, she came face-to-face with Paulo. She grasped the newel and blinked.

"Good day." Paulo bowed deeply. "You have been visiting Miss Alcester?"

"Yes." Lucy looked around, wishing someone would come.

Paulo's teeth flashed in an understanding smile. "The family is occupied elsewhere, so I must introduce myself. I am, Miss Chalmers, Paulo da Silva. May I escort you to your steed?"

"You know me?"

"Young Peter said you were here." Paulo crooked his arm, and Lucy placed trembling fingers on it. "Is it true you and Mr. Robert wish to wed, but are forbidden to do so?" he asked politely.

Lucy stiffened. How dare he ask such personal questions? She hadn't a notion how to answer.

He said, "I've embarrassed you, have I not? You must forgive me. I have yet to learn just what one may speak of openly and when one must creep around corners on tippytoes merely touching on the subject."

Paulo helped Lucy up into her saddle. She hooked her knee firmly and settled her skirts. Then she really looked at Paulo. She saw a kind face and dark, warm eyes. She couldn't help but smile back when he smiled at her. Impulsively, she held her hand down to him, and he grasped it. "It is a very private and personal matter, sir, but I'll answer you because I believe you wish us well. Robert and I would like to marry, but at the moment there are difficulties. We'll come about in the end. I'm sure of it."

"Your father wishes you to marry well?"

She sighed. "I'm sure it is the way of all fathers. Good day."

Paulo watched her go before searching out Secundus. "She is a nice little thing," he said. Sec looked blank. "Robert's Miss Chalmers. She would do very well for him, I think."

"You do, do you?"

"I think her father is not aware of all the ramifications"—Paulo rolled the word off his tongue with a touch of justified pride—"of marrying into the honored family of the elder Alcester. He forbids the match."

"He does, does he?" Sec looked up from the letter he'd been doing his best to decipher. "Robert isn't good enough for his little girl?"

"It is not, I believe, that Robert isn't good enough for a precious daughter. It's more that he is not wealthy enough."

"Paulo, you're a cynical soul." Sec's eyes narrowed, and the cynicism sounded in his voice. "Surely Chalmers wouldn't blight love's young joy for the want of a few pounds in the three percents?"

"But it seems that he would, oh honored second son."

"Then," sighed Secundus, "I suppose I'd best go about setting up the trusts for my relatives. If I read this rightly"—he waved the letter—"I must go to London anyway. You've been asking about the London office. Now you may see for yourself why I'll find it a dead bore."

"Often and often we've discovered that what you find a bore I find quite interesting," soothed Paulo. "Perhaps this is another such case."

Secundus studied Paulo's face. It was perfectly bland, the eyes steady and giving nothing away, but Secundus's suspicions were roused. "Hmmm." Paulo's teeth flashed in a grin. "Hmmhumm. I see." Paulo tipped his head, questioningly. "Well, *perhaps* I see . . . Poor Gubby," Sec added, his eyes twinkling. "He arrives today and we must tell him we leave for London one day very soon. The man will be quite bewildered by such antics."

"You may tell him you require him to be responsible for your family while we are gone."

"Perhaps I will just to see his look of horror. What fun." Secundus handed Paulo the letter. "See what you make of those hen scratches. I can't read the half of it." They reached a conclusion concerning the business just as the forecourt filled with such racket it drew them into the hall.

Sir Augustus Falconer had arrived. He drove a curricle, with a tiger on the step. Following, was a closed carriage from which an upper servant descended, his nose quite out of joint at the lack of pretension in the house to which they'd come. Then came a more serviceable carriage for the baggage. Behind that was a long dray pulled by six sturdy beasts and filled to capacity with boxes and bundles of all shapes and sizes. Secundus took one look and doubled over laughing. He controlled himself, took another look, and, weakened by more laughter, turned to lean against the door frame.

The children ran down the stairs. The little girls reached for the security of Paulo's hands, but Peter took one look at the carriages, horses, and men, and raced back up the stairs, shouting, "Ruth will have a tizzy fit." Robert came around the side of the house. He realized the chubby man climbing down from the curricle must be his uncle's friend and strode forward, a welcome on his tongue, but he, too, wondered what they'd do with the men, horses, and carriages, to say nothing of the pile of boxes, crates, barrels, and bundles on the long wagon.

"Yes, yes, glad to meet you m'boy," said Sir Augustus,

his glowering gaze on Sec, who was manfully trying to contain chuckles and not succeeding. "I suddenly remember one of the things which irritated me about your uncle, son. He always laughed at all the wrong things at all the wrong moments and did it more often than anyone I've ever known."

"Gubby, ol' friend," demanded Sec between chortles, "did you lead that parade all the way from London?"

"I did not. The wagon must have gone off several days ago to be here now, as you very well know. I met it at the gate."

"I can't think what all you've got there," said Sec coming on down the steps. He rubbed his nose. "I ordered a few things, but not all that!"

"Your order," said Sir Augustus testily, "arrives within the hour. I passed it this side of Lewes. That," he said, waving a languid hand toward the dray, "is from India. Personal items for which your factor in London cannot take it on himself to be responsible. Or so he insisted when he came, hat in hand, to see me. I had no notion where to put it." He eyed Sec, awaiting another bout of chuckles.

"Do I detect a touch of bitterness?"

"Now why should I be bitter when I'm not one of your native lads, existing for no other purpose than to run to your beck and call?"

"By Ol' Nick's nightgown! I see that you're seriously upset." Sec put his arm around his friend and drew him into the shabby but comfortable parlor. "Now you just settle right here and I'll pour you up a glass of this very fine claret which I found in Lewes—properly sealed by a customs agent, I assure you," he added when the glass was given a suspicious glare.

"Sec," said Augustus after a moment and in a more benign tone, "I believe I'll survive." He added on a confiding note, "Never did travel well, you'll remember. So. If you will tell me where I may find my valet, and, assuming the house runs to a bath," he added, with another faintly irritated look around the shabby room, "I'll retire and make myself presentable." He looked at his nails and sighed. "I do hope I've some time before this garden party to which you tell me we're invited. Who will our host be?"

"Rotherford, you know."

Augustus's brows arced. "Rotherford, you say? Forgot he had a place here. Seem to remember . . ." As his voice trailed off, his gaze flicked toward Sec, then away. He blinked and stared down at the pure jewel-like color of his wine.

"Remember another reason why I always liked you," said Sec, warmly. "Never probed where it might hurt, did you?" The baronet looked shocked at the very notion. Sec smiled. "You're a good man, Gubby," he said warmly. "Helen and I will get it right this time, and there'll be no interference." Augustus looked a question and Sec shrugged. "She'll not allow it."

"Well, if it's Rotherford's party, it's imperative I put myself in the hands of my valet. Should do the pretty by my hostess first," he hinted.

Secundus looked slightly rattled. "Suppose that is the proper thing to do, isn't it? Being away from England so long, I've forgotten." He sighed. "Come along. We'll find Ruth and see what she's arranged."

Ruth had things in hand. The valet and baggage had been shown to the rooms prepared for Sir Augustus, a connecting one put into service as a dressing room. But she'd winced at the load of wax-sealed barrels, heavy crates, and the awkward bundles which had been sewn into heavy canvas, leaking straw at the seams. It was a formidable quantity of goods. The first of it was being carried up the stairs to a rarely used lady's parlor quickly prepared to receive it. Sec and Sir Augustus found her there.

"What is all this, Uncle Sec?" she asked after greeting Sir Augustus and tactfully dismissing him to his room. She stared at a particularly oddly shaped item.

Secundus, usually clear, concise, and to the point, mumbled, "Oh, this and that. Nothing important, I suppose. *Be careful with that!*" he finished as one of the men dropped a box. "You go on now," he said to Ruth, "and I'll oversee. That barrel goes by the door—I might want to get into it," he interrupted himself. "Those crates can go against the back wall," he said to another man. "Now let's get organized here," he finished testily and waved away Ruth's offers of aid. "Can't tolerate disorder," he said, "so listen well. That trunk . . ."

Ruth dodged still another man and found herself face-to-face with the baronet's supercilious valet. "May I help you?" she asked.

"Sir Augustus requires the bath," she was told, a stern eye making her feel very much an erring child. "Immediately. Don't dawdle, missy."

Ruth's lips twitched and her eyes twinkled. "Oi'll do me best," she said, and berated herself for allowing her sense of humor too much freedom. The valet would be vexed with himself when he discovered he'd mistaken the mistress for the maid. But a spurt of laughter lightened her mood.

Ruth gave orders for the bath and hot water to be sent up and was summoned to the kitchen to greet the driver of a second, much smaller, wagon, bearing her uncle's purchases. Once she'd sorted out the clothing and sent it to Secundus's room, she was left with wine, a large supply of wax candles, huge hams, several cheeses and other food. That she could deal with competently.

When she went up to dress, it occurred to her she was

looking forward to the party, that for once she'd not spent the entire day worrying about what she might say to Rotherford and what he might reply. She wasn't, already, all to pieces, having imagined every possible contretemps and embarrassing possibility. With luck, she might, she thought, manage two words with her host without blushing.

After all, she'd spoken like a sensible person the last two times they'd met, so why not again? Perhaps she might even attempt a little in the way of light flirtation. Now that was an intriguing thought. Ruth had forgotten they'd parted last on less than the best of terms.

Secundus, dressing, wasn't happy with his new cravat. It was wider than those to which he was accustomed and refused to behave. Taking up another of the starched neck-cloths, he went down the hall. "Gubby?" His friend made a shushing sound at him. Sec slid on into the room and stood quietly. He blinked as the valet threw another cravat on the pile littering the floor. "By Ol' Nick's neckerchief, surely it—" He broke off when he was shushed again, this time by both valet and master.

It took three more attempts before Augustus was satisfied. Even then, the valet frowned and poked at a pleat here and touched up a crease there. "Away with you man, it'll do. Nothing but country folk, I'll be bound. No one who will tell tales among our friends. Now that's enough," insisted Gubby. "The coat, man."

The coat was forced over his shoulders, the struggle leading to an irrepressible chuckle from Secundus. "See you don't need any extra exercise these days," he said. "Just getting into your clothes must be enough for any man." He frowned. "Here now, Weston didn't make my coats that tight, did he? I'll have the man's ears if he did."

"You never had a notion of proper style," said Sir Augustus with a touch of scorn. "But Weston will have taken your measure in more ways than the obvious and you'll find the coats suit you very well." Gubby went to the dressing table and seated himself. "The brutus, don't you think?" he asked his valet who was fussing with brushes and combs.

"Exactly right, sir. You have, as usual, chosen the proper style for the day," said the valet, far more snobbish than his master.

"Well, get on with it. Why did you come to my room, Sec?"

"Well, I thought I wished help with my cravat, but if I have to have a couple of dozen to work with each day, we'll forget the whole thing. I'll tie a kerchief around my neck like a stagecoach driver does."

"And perhaps file your teeth to points as well?"

"Now why would I wish to do anything so stupid?"

"It's what those aping the coachees do."

Secundus stared.

"I'm serious. It's all the crack among some of the wilder young men. What sort of cravat do you wish to achieve?"

"I want the blasted thing tied around my neck."

"But what style? Mine, for instance, is in the mathematical."

Secundus was silent for a moment. "Gubby?"

"Yes, Sec?" Sir Augustus was staring into the mirror, frowning slightly. "Isn't it just a trifle too long there?" He pointed toward his left ear.

"A trifle, perhaps. Should I trim it, sir?"

"Have we time?"

"Gubby!"

"Oh. Sorry, Sec."

"Something simple. I'm a simple man, after all."

Augustus put up his hands and stopped the valet from fussing with his hair. Then he turned and looked at Sec. "Oh. The cravat. Simple, you say?" Sec blushed. "Well, well. Twinner, do you see? I believe it is a matter of *l'amour*!"

"Yes, sir. I will do what I can, sir." He laid down the comb and scissors. "Now, Mr. Alcester, if you'd be so good as to stand just here. And, now sir, if you'd tip your head just a trifle higher . . . and that's right, sir, lower your chin slowly. Slowly, sir." The valet jabbed at a fold. "Just a bit more. Enough. I do believe that's entirely right, sir."

Secundus stood absolutely still, only his gaze moving from the valet to his friend and back again. "Hmmm," said Sir Augustus.

"I think—" started the pleased valet.

"But—" began his master, frowning.

"Or maybe—" interrupted the man, seeing the problem. He darted forward, tugged at one crease, deepened another. He tipped his head.

Sir Augustus rose from his seat and approached. He looked at the cravat from several angles. "You've done it, Twinner, and at the very first try."

"It is a miracle." The valet clasped his hands.

"Can I talk?" asked Secundus barely moving his jaw.

"Of course you can talk. Why shouldn't you?"

"For fear of disarranging the thing."

"No, no. Once it is set, then of course it is there to stay. Now go away, Secundus. We must have silence to achieve just the proper style."

"You've become a popinjay."

"So I have. So I have. Now, away with you so I may get on with it. We'll talk some other time. Nothing is more important than dressing when one is dressing. One makes oneself perfect, then, according to Brummel, one should forget all about it, you know. Now go."

Shaking his head in disgust, Sec returned to his own room where he stared at the coat laid out on his bed. It had better be looser than the one he'd watched his old friend struggle into. He'd done quite all right without a valet in India, and he'd hoped to continue doing so now he was home, but fashion had changed a great deal. He moved to the mirror where he checked the cravat. He poked at one of the creases and tugged lightly at the ends of the knot. It was the ugliest cravat he'd ever seen, but Gubby thought it perfect, so perhaps Helen would think so, too.

The coat required only a bit of effort. Sec was reasonably well satisfied. He took another look at the cravat and snorted. Would Gubby be insulted if he ripped it off and tried another, simpler, style? He remembered the mess he'd made when he *had* tried and sighed in resignation. Maybe he wouldn't propose today after all. Helen would more than likely be too distracted by the monstrosity around his neck to pay proper attention to anything so mundane as a proposal.

Ten

Helen, greeting guests near the front of the house, was trapped by a garrulous dowager. She could do no more than look up when still another carriage arrived. She was relieved it was not the gentleman whom she awaited.

The baron stood somewhat farther along the path toward the gardens. He, too, waited impatiently for one particular arrival. Ruth Alcester was becoming an obsession. Why couldn't he decide what to do about her? It seemed he'd always known that when the time came, he'd choose a wife from among those presented at Almack's, a proper young miss who would be approved by his family and friends. So why was he actually contemplating offering for Miss Alcester? How could he account for the fact he was attracted to a woman well past the first blush of youth, who was neither a diamond nor a sophisticated woman he'd trust to understand the rules of a mere flirtation?

Ruth Alcester was not a type he'd ever found interesting. She was too innocent. She was too tall for a woman and too well endowed. He smiled at his next thought: very likely she'd add a modicum of weight with the years and become a dowager of near-overpowering character, a leader of whatever society she graced. . . . And, he thought catching sight of her in a very pretty yellow dress, she'd grace today very well indeed! He turned on his heel and walked away.

"She's here," said Rotherford to his nephew.

"Who? Oh." Gerry's frown lightened. "The Alcesters have arrived."

"Don't look quite so much like a puppy who smells a treat."

"Don't sound quite so much like a cook who, spoon in hand, will forbid it."

John's bark of laughter drew eyes. Why had he drawn Gerry's attention to the Alcesters' arrival? "I thought you decided to toddle up to London this autumn," he said as idly as he could.

"I have."

"Then don't arouse expectations where you've no intentions."

"The boot's on the other foot, you know," confided Gerry.

John felt icy fingers walk around inside him. "Which foot?" he asked, then kicked himself for such an inane response. "What can you mean?"

Gerry grinned reminiscently. "Tibby proposed to me."

"Gerry," said John impatiently, "I wasn't talking about the child."

Gerry stared. "You mean Miss Alcester?" He blinked. "She doesn't play the sort of game in which I'm interested just now. I tried flirting with her one day, and she hadn't a notion what it's all about. For my tastes, she is too lacking in guile—much too honest and far too unsophisticated."

"A paragon in fact," said John, his eyes searching the garden for another glimpse of that particular paragon.

"Yes, I think she very well may be."

John threw a sidelong glance toward Gerry. The simple phrase carried more weight than the longest, best-planned argument. "You've been too long with the army," he insisted. "You've forgotten what women are like."

"Not so. The fact is, you've associated with the wrong women for so long, you've forgotten there is more than one kind." Gerry glanced John's way, but saw only stubbornness. "Think of your sister. What of Miss Brown?" He cast about for another example. "Or Chalmers's daughter?"

John smiled, but there was a sour twist to his lips. "You shouldn't have mentioned Miss Chalmers. You forget, she's sequestered in her room in an attempt to manipulate her father. She is cozening her father and will treat all men with whom she deals in a like manner."

"You'll go on to say Miss Brown and Helen manipulate us?"

Rotherford's lips compressed again. He nodded. "I believe they do. It is only that they use less common methods and are more subtle about it."

"Of course you never manipulate a woman."

"Me? Why should I have to?"

Gerry laughed at the hurt arrogance obvious in high-nosed tone and stance. "I've no notion why, but you do, John. Wasn't this party a plot to bring your sister home and into Society for a bit?"

"But that is for her own good."

"I see." Gerry nodded sagely. "When you do it, it is for someone's good. If a woman does it, any woman, for any reason, then it must, by the fact of it, be bad."

John felt his ears heat. "You needn't make me sound a coxcomb."

"You should know better than to make generalizations about women any more than you do about men, John. You'll never find happiness that way."

Rotherford's brows arched. "Happiness? Don't become maudlin, Ger, or I'll cut our acquaintance."

Gerry shook his head in mock disgust. Rotherford, watching the younger man stroll away, pursed his lips at his own stubborn nature. Why had he nearly bitten off Gerry's head? It wasn't as if he truly believed all women were the same, but he'd felt it necessary to argue the notion with Gerry. He was, he thought wryly and with new self-knowledge, very like a drowning man grasping at straws. Were all men in such a dither when they contemplated the possibility they might, per chance, have come to it and were—horrible thought—about to ask the women of their choice The Question?

Looking around for distraction, John noticed Ruth Alcester strolling with Sir Augustus Falconer. What was that man-milliner saying to make Miss Alcester laugh that way? Weren't her cheeks a trifle flushed? Was the old court-card talking a trifle warmly, saying things he shouldn't to an innocent country woman? And how had she come to meet the man? Rotherford moved to greet them.

"Ah. Rotherford. Splendid day. Just splendid," said Sir Augustus.

Ruth's head came up. Then her gaze dropped to the path. Rotherford watched her chin firm before her face was again raised, her candid eyes meeting his. "My lord," she said in an even tone.

"Good afternoon Miss Alcester." Then hoping to please her, he added, "May I say how well you look."

"Yes. Amazing what new feathers can do for an old bird." Her eyes widened slightly and she flushed rosily, her eyes darting to meet his questioning gaze, thereby giving away the fact she was aware *bird* was a cant term for a woman. A certain type of woman. "Oh dear."

"Not so very old, Miss Alcester," said Sir Augustus.

Simultaneously, John said, "Fine feathers only look fine on fine birds."

Ruth's face flamed. "Please, my lord, Sir Augustus, I wasn't fishing. Don't feel you must perjure yourselves." Both men broke into protests, assuring her of their sincerity, and Ruth's hands flew to cover her cheeks. "I only make bad worse, do I not? May we change the subject since the ground refuses to open and allow me to sink into it?"

Rotherford paused and, head to one side, studied her. He concluded she was not pretending, but was truly embarrassed. At least the ice had been broken and they were talking, so he obligingly changed the subject. "You must be pleased your uncle has returned from abroad," he said. Then he wondered if that would be another sore point between them, since he'd approached her to discover what he could of that same uncle's finances. Relief flooded him when her eyes lit up.

"Dear Uncle Secundus. Tibby insists he's come as a direct result of her catching her genie and making his arrival one of the chores the genie was to do for her."

"Have you heard how she came to confuse Gerry with a genie?" asked Rotherford, grasping the chance to amuse her.

Ruth laughed at his description of the trousers. Sir Augustus denigrated them as a mistake which Petersham, their designer, stubbornly refused to admit. He then insisted on the whole story about the genie. Rotherford listened to Ruth's playful account, smiled at the small jokes she made, and was surprised to discover he was enjoying himself a great deal.

Too much, perhaps? Was levity the correct state of mind for a man on the verge of a momentous decision?

Using the excuse that he must circulate, he left Ruth to the dubious honor of Sir Augustus's escort. The man was a friend, it seemed, of Secundus, and, as such, one must presume, to be trusted, but just in case he was not, John sent Gerry along to play gooseberry.

Even then he didn't allow Ruth to move completely out of his ken. He knew where she was every moment. The woman was deucedly intriguing. Once she'd controlled her embarrassment, she'd talked and joked and amused him like a sensible woman. And there was no denying that he was attracted by her form. Why had Ruth—Miss Alcester—not revealed that playful side until recently?

The answer came unexpectedly quickly as he watched a very young maiden, blushing and tongue-tied, at the advances of an equally young man, but woebegone when he left her side. Had Ruth Alcester once been infatuated and unable to face him? But, if that were the case, then her recent ease of manner would indicate Miss Alcester had recovered from her infatuation. What had brought that about?

She'd met Gerry, of course.

"Well, John?" Helen came up to him and put her arm through his, leading him toward the rose garden. "Are you p-p-pleased?"

"As usual, you've done very well, Helen."

"But something's bothering you."

He glanced down at her profile. "You were always able to read me."

"Having read," she said in her dry way, "I wish an answer. Tell me."

John sighed. "You'll tell me I deserve it."

"It?"

"To suffer under the burden of an unrequited love," he declaimed. Making light of his answer, he postured, head turned, back of hand to forehead, and heaved a deep soulful sigh.

"Ruth Alcester?"

John snapped back to normal. "How the devil . . . ?"

Helen shook her head. "Come, John, I have eyes and ears and I know you. But wherein lies the p-p-problem?" He motioned to where Gerry strolled with Ruth on his arm, Tibby holding his free hand. "Gerry? He bought his commission before he'd sowed a single wild oat and, whatever he may have got up to while with the army, he has never had a grass time here in England. He'll go to Brighton soon or London and play—the way young men do."

"He's very taken with Ruth Alcester despite his denials."

"He's very with Tibby Alcester and he makes no pretense of it."

John frowned. "Tibby is a child."

"Therefore beneath notice?"

"Have *you* ever been interested in one?"

"Y–y-yes. More than one." John was sensitive to his sister's moods, too. He touched her hand. "I'm thirty-four, John." She walked another few paces before stopping, asking, diffidently, "John, am I too old to have ch-ch-children?"

"Helen, how should I know something like that?"

"I worry I can't give Secundus a son."

"Ahem." The voice came from the other side of the statue beside which they stood talking. Helen swung around. "Well now, Helen," said Secundus, "I wouldn't put myself forward into what I perceived to be a private conversation, but it's come around to *our* needing privacy." Secundus stared at John. "You are very much *de trop,* m'lad."

John hadn't been called lad in a long, long time. He grinned. "Do I recall your telling me you have a habit of putting your foot in it?"

"Hm?" Sec had his mind on his love.

"Lad, indeed. Well, never mind. Helen, I haven't a notion what you see in this . . . this . . . *him.* Just be very careful he isn't after your fortune." Aha, thought John, that brought the man's attention back to him.

"Helen's fortune may be tied up any way you please. We won't need it."

"Sec, you don't have a notion of my needs," said Helen sharply.

"We'll settle your monies on you and you may play ducks and drakes with them if you like, m'love, but will you tell your overprotective brother to go away so we may talk about this other thing?"

"John, go away."

"So you may talk about the other thing?" John grinned. "Alcester, are you serious about not needing Helen's fortune?"

"What in hades do you think I've up to in India? By Ol' Nick's nostrils, I don't have a notion what you call a fortune, but believe me I can support a wife. Even a Rotherford wife."

"Very well. I believe you."

"John," said Helen as he was about to turn away.

"Yes?"

"Gerry is not in love with Miss Alcester."

"But is she with him?"

"You forget," said Secundus, "I overheard that conversation." He adopted an outrageously stern manner which made Rotherford stiffen even as he noted the twinkling eyes. "What, my boy, are your intentions toward my eldest niece?" he asked portentously, his finger extended and rudely pointing.

"I've not decided," said Rotherford, wavering between outrage and a desire to laugh. The laughter won, but also a trifling need for revenge. "If I conclude they're dishonorable, I'll be sure you never hear of it."

"In that case, we've no problem, have we?"

Rotherford, finding he didn't like such a casual attitude toward the woman he'd been forced to admit meant a great deal to him, scowled.

"If I don't hear of it," Sec continued, "I assure you no one else will either. Then it, whatever it is, is between the two of you. Just make certain of that or you will have problems, won't you?"

"I'm an honorable man, Alcester."

"And my niece is an honorable woman, but, at twenty-four, she's well beyond any man's guardianship. Her brothers wouldn't agree, of course," he said as an obvious afterthought.

"How did we get into such a disagreeable discussion?" asked Helen. "My brother has no intention of seducing Miss Alcester."

John cocked an eye her way. "Are you certain of that?" he asked, his features a bland mask.

"John, don't give Sec a wrong impression of you."

"Why not? He's done his best to give us a wrong impression of himself, hasn't he?"

"I have?" asked Sec cautiously.

"Haven't you?" asked John.

Sec rubbed his nose. "Well, now . . ."

"Never mind. I won't say a word. You may go on playing your little games if you wish to."

Secundus watched John walk off. Helen, nobody's fool, jerked at his sleeve. "Secundus Alcester, did you come back from India a nabob?"

"Does it make any difference," he asked cautiously.

"Of course it does. Why, think of the schools and orphanages and . . . oh, everything I might do with a nabob's fortune."

Secundus eyed her. "Helen, I only said you may do as you please with your monies. Didn't say a word about letting you do as you please with mine."

She hugged his arm. "But you did, Sec. Have you forgotten? I distinctly remember you telling me you'd support me in anything I wished to do." She skipped a step or two just as a much younger girl might do. Her face was flushed with laughter. "And I thought you meant moral support."

"Well, now. What makes you think I meant anything else?"

She poked a finger in his ribs. "You're a tease, but, Sec," she added more soberly, "the problem of an heir won't go away for wishing."

He turned her to face him. "Helen, Helen, do you think I care for such things? In fact, mightn't it be better if you don't conceive? I've waited so long for you and I'll be damned if"—her left brow rose at the word—"yes, Helen, I'll be *damned* if I lose you in child-bed merely for the sake of an heir. Besides, I have heirs. We'll borrow the young ones and, once babies start arriving, our great-nieces and nephews—a large family for us without endangering you, if that's all right with you?" he finished on a more tentative note. "Oh, Helen, don't cry. What have I said to make you cry?" He tipped up her face to wipe her cheeks.

"Are you sure you don't want children of your own?" she asked.

"I fear I'm a trifle old to put up with the little darlings. Now there's a good thing—if we *borrow* them, we may give them back when we tire of them."

"Sec, Sec," she said attempting to stay serious, but joining almost immediately with his chuckles. The subject wasn't settled to Helen's satisfaction, but she realized that a garden filled with friends and neighbors was no place for a full-blown discussion.

In another part of the extensive gardens Rotherford strolled with Ruth, who showed not a whisper of a partiality for himself. She was wonderfully serene, except when in one of her humorous moods. He couldn't decide which trait was most to his taste. He was on the verge of taking the plunge and proposing . . . if only she would show the slightest sign she'd welcome his addresses.

"Well, Lord Rotherford, I'm not certain whether . . . ," she began after a thoughtful pause in response to a question he'd already forgotten he'd asked.

He touched her hand where it lay on his arm, interrupting her. She looked up at him, questioningly. "I've an ambition," he said, "to hear my name on your lips." She didn't respond and he glanced under the parasol, found she was peering up at him, a dimple playing hide and seek in her flushed cheek. "Yes?"

She shook her head. "No. Impossible." But the dimple suggested she was controlling laughter.

"I have several from which you may choose," he hinted.

"I wouldn't wish to take liberties, my lord."

"Fulfilling my wishes is hardly taking liberties." She twirled her parasol and said nothing. Playing the buffoon for the second time that day, John bowed with a certain hauteur. "Allow me to introduce John Hubert Longford Rotherford." She still said nothing, but the dimple made further playful appearance. "Won't you choose from such an embarrassing number of names, m'dear?"

"I had a kitten once named Bertie," she offered. He winced. Hubee was bad, but Bertie was, he decided, even worse. "I loved that kitten," she said with seeming irrelevance.

He pictured her holding it, petting it, allowing it to snuggle against her breast and under her chin. How utterly ridiculous to feel jealousy toward a kitten which, long ago, had grown to be a cat. "Perhaps I wouldn't mind being likened to a kitten if it were one loved by you."

She glanced at him and the dimple disappeared. "Lord Rotherford."

"You were to choose a name." He turned her, his hands holding her just above the elbows. The very tips of her fingers touched his waistcoat, held him away from her.

"This makes us appear quite singular, my lord. Please release me."

"We'd not look at all odd if you were a member of my family."

Her eyes widened, the pupils dilating, almost obscuring the color. "But I'm not."

"But you could be." Rotherford blinked twice. Had he actually done that? Had he proposed?

"Lord Roth—"

"John," he interrupted. "Say it, Ruth." Her given name slipped out without his realizing.

"John," she responded obediently, but added with severity, "I think you've been too long in the sun."

He threw back his head and laughed, but sobered quickly enough. "Do you say that because I've proposed to you?"

"Is that what you did? I thought you were offering to adopt me." She tossed her head and looked away to hide the dampness in her eyes. A girl dreamed of her first proposal and this was not at all as it should be.

"Now my dear, don't go off in a distempered freak. Surely you don't expect me to get down on my knee here in the knot garden with half the neighborhood in sight?"

She bit her lip, her gaze searching his. She saw that special warmth there. The warmth faded, and the only name she could put to what she read then was insecurity.

Rotherford? Insecure? Was he truly worried? Except it *had* been a rather off-hand proposal. For an instant, she'd thought him as stunned by it as she'd been herself. In fact, she was nearly sure of it. "My lord . . ."

"Drat it, Ruth, will you, at the very least, stop m'lord-ing me?" Her lips compressed; the dimples formed. He touched the left one. "Ruth? Don't say me nay. Perhaps, as I think you guessed, I'd not intended asking you today. But I have been thinking of it. It wasn't just the sun or your pretty new dress. I enjoy your company, Ruth, and your conversation. I admire you very much for a great number of excellent qualities. Will you forget we've had this conversation and go on today as we have been, and someday soon I'll make my offer again and in proper form?" His fingers tightened very slightly on her arms.

Ruth stared at him. The tension around his eyes caused a myriad tiny lines. They were barely visible but they were there. He *was* concerned. She bit her lip. "My lo—John, I don't know what to say."

"Don't say anything. Another time I'll ask you prop-erly, m'dear, and then you may answer me."

"My lor—John, will you think me a harum-scarum lit-tle madam if I ask that you not repeat your offer immediately? That you give me time to get to know you better?" Time, she thought, for you to know me and all my faults and bad points.

"You are the only woman to whom I've ever felt the least desire to propose. I'll do whatever is necessary to make myself acceptable to you. For now, we'll go on as if this interlude never occurred. Simply remember, m'dear, give me the slightest sign you'll answer as I hope you will and I'll be on my knee to you, even if we're in the middle of a cotillion at a ball given by Prinny at the Pavilion!"

"I can see it now," she responded, relaxing slightly as he turned and led her back toward more populated parts of the garden. "All the ladies in their finery with brightly sparkling jewels. The men in their dancing pumps and best waistcoats. The chandeliers glittering brightly. And there you'll be, my—John. The light will reflect off your bent head and make me blink. I won't know where to look. Tears of mortification will blind me, and some kind soul will lead me off the floor." They laughed at the picture she drew. "Oh, dear me," she said when she could speak again. "No, I don't think you'd better do that."

"Then, at a sign, I'll find a proper moment. Will that do?"

Ruth sobered. "I can't promise the sign will ever come."

"Why? Am I so repugnant to you?" he asked bluntly.

"No." She said it quite as baldly, firmly controlling wild thoughts of accepting him before he could change his mind. "No," she repeated. "It certainly isn't that. But you are a peer and I a mere commoner." Her eyes widened. "Oh, *worse*, my lord—I'm the destitute daughter of a scandal-making father. I fear you've not thought of all the ramifications of what I'm quite certain was the impulse of the moment—one you're already regretting."

"No regrets. None. I've never understood why children must suffer for their father's sins. Put the scandal from your mind, Ruth. It is forgotten by anyone who counts. What other objections have you, since you appear to be unwilling to put it away for now and simply enjoy the day?"

She glanced away from him. "I must for now, must I not? It wouldn't do for this conversation to be overheard. But there are a few questions which must be answered. How you feel about my responsibility for my sisters, for instance, and the fact that I have no dowry. I am not a suitable bride for you, my lord. Oh dear, there's Tibby. How worried she looks. Tibby!"

"There you are. Marie is in tears. Please come."

"Where is she?"

"I've left her with my genie. Do hurry, Ruth. She won't stop."

Rotherford followed. He'd remembered he must get to know the children, particularly the one called Tibby. If Gerry were correct, it was not impossible that Ruth would deny his suit merely because the child took him in dislike. How did one get to know a child? He caught up with them as the girl led Ruth into the mazelike plantings around the pavilion. There they found Gerry holding Marie, who sobbed, heartbroken, leaning into Gerry's coat as if he were her sole support.

"What has happened? Are you hurt, my love?" asked Ruth going down on her knees before them and taking Marie's hands into her own. Marie simply stared at her, hiccuping softly, the tears running down her cheeks. "Tibby? What has happened?"

"I don't know," said the older child on a note of exasperation. "I can't get her to say anything either. And the tears just flow and flow."

"Marie, love, please tell me." Seating herself, Ruth took the child into her lap. "We love you and we want you to be happy. You know that."

Marie's tears soaked into her dress, and Ruth felt a guilty wish her youngest sister would not spoil her pretty new gown. The child's hot face pressed against her, and when she continued to refuse to answer, Ruth said, "Tibby, love, you'd better ask Robert to harness the landau so I may take Marie home. When she's like this it may take forever to discover what is bothering her."

Tibby nodded. "I'll come back when I've found

Robert." The lieutenant offered to help find Marie's brother and followed her. Rotherford stared helplessly at the tableau of woman and child. What could he do?

"Come child," said Ruth. "Here is Lord Rotherford. See how worried he is about you?" She turned Marie's face up. The child blinked. Remembering how ladies cooed at babies, Rotherford made a face at her. Her eyes widened. He contorted his features in another way. Marie put her finger in her mouth. Ruth, who had been watching her sister, looked up. Rotherford immediately looked away, whistling softly. Ruth frowned, but worried about Marie, looked back down. "Can you say good day, Lord Rotherford?"

"Day," mumbled Marie around her finger. The child made a face and watched Rotherford with interest. He made one back and she responded.

Ruth blinked, looked up at Rotherford, but didn't catch on to what he was doing. "Marie . . ." Marie giggled, ducked her still hot face into her sister's dress again, peeking up at the man. This time when Ruth looked up it was to see one of Rotherford's grimaces. Her mouth fell open, but he shook his head slightly, continuing to trade expressions with Marie.

When Tibby returned, she had Peter and Secundus with her. Marie was chuckling softly, although her eyes were still bright with tears. Tibby gaped.

Ruth, noticing, laughed. "I'm sorry I sent you off, Tibby, love."

"Discovered what is bothering her?" asked Sec.

Marie was looking tired now, drooping in Ruth's arms. "I haven't been able to get a word out of her, but at least Lord Rotherford stopped her crying." Ruth smiled up at him and Rotherford, much to his disgust, felt himself flush.

At that moment Robert and Gerry arrived. "Give her to me, Ruth," said her brother. "I know of no reason why we must all have our day ruined. I can deal with her when she's in one of her states at least as well as you can, so you mustn't worry about her. Ralston has offered to drive us to the manor and to bring the rig back. Now no argument, Ruth. You've looked forward to this day and I've no special reason for being here." He took Marie up and started off. Marie lay her head against his shoulder, half asleep already.

Ruth looked after them. What had happened to turn Marie into such a watering pot? Most often her tears were prompted by a misunderstanding, the child convinced her small world was to turn upside down. It was true that when that happened, Robert often had a better touch with her. Taking Tibby's hand she began to walk out of the maze. "Have you no notion at all what happened, Tibby?"

"No. She was playing with some other little girls." Tibby scowled. "Everything was all right. Truly. Then, suddenly she ran over and threw her arms around me the way she does and was crying all over me."

Tibby's words were a trifle caustic, but Ruth knew she hid a deep concern. "Robert will take care of her. He took her so the rest of us might continue to enjoy ourselves. Promise me you will?"

Tibby glowered for a moment. Then she sighed. "Yes. Robert would be unhappy with us, wouldn't he, if we don't trust him with her."

"Exactly."

Tibby sighed hugely. "I suppose I'd better apologize to Peter."

"Why must you do that?" she asked cautiously.

"Because I called him names when he didn't know where Robert was."

"I'm sorry I was mad at you," Peter said handsomely. "Besides, you were partly right. I was acting like a silly care-for-nobody."

"Does that mean," asked Tibby, innocently, "I only need to apologize for calling you a rakeshame?"

Ruth looked from one to the other. Care-for-nobody? Rakeshame? Her eyes sought Rotherford's, and she saw he was attempting to hide a grin.

Peter glared at his younger sister. "You most certainly must. I'm not old enough to be a rakeshame."

"What *is* a rakeshame?" asked Tibby.

"Never you mind," said Peter, throwing a red-faced look toward Ruth and a harassed one toward Rotherford. "Just don't go calling anyone it, or you'll find yourself in queer street."

"Queer street?" asked Tibby and Peter groaned. "What does *that* mean?"

"Ruth will explain," he said with an apologetic look to his eldest sister. "Just you remember, don't you go using words like that, you hear?" Turning to Ruth he added, "If we're staying I'm returning to the tennis court."

Ruth nodded and, with a bow to Rotherford, he ran off before Tibby could again ask why. The little girl turned to Ruth with her mouth open. Ruth shook her head, but there was a twinkle in her eyes, and Tibby knew her sister was amused. "Was it so very bad," asked the child.

"Very. Peter is right. You must not use such words."

"But I heard them from—"

Ruth stopped her by the simple expedient of covering her lips with one firm finger. "It matters not who said them, Tibby. What matters is that you were listening when you weren't supposed to, were you not?" Tibby hung her head, the toe of one shoe digging into the gravel but her mouth compressed into a well-known stubborn line. "Tibby, what am I to do with you?"

"Good afternoon, my lord. Miss Alcester. Have we trouble?"

"Miss Brown," Ruth sighed. "Oh, dear, just when one would most wish to be elsewhere. We don't want you to get a poor impression of your pupil."

Miss Brown greeted the adults, then looked at Tibby. "What have you been up to, child?" she asked, holding out her hand. "Come along and tell me about it."

"You won't scold?"

"Should I scold?"

"Very likely," said Tibby, putting her hand in Miss Brown's. She walked away earnestly explaining about how she'd heard words Peter and Ruth said she wasn't to use and how she wasn't supposed to listen to other people's conversations, but often she learned very important things that way, so . . .

"So that's Tibby," said Rotherford when child and governess were beyond hearing. "*Does* Tibby eavesdrop?"

"It's her besetting sin. And nothing I've done breaks her of it. She merely responds, quite patiently, that she must listen or she won't learn."

"Miss Brown will sort her out."

"I hope so." Ruth glanced down at her gown and noticed how crushed it had become and that her kneeling had dirtied the skirt.

Rotherford noticed, too. "Aha. An opportunity to play the knight errant, my dear, and put myself in your good graces. Follow me."

"Where?"

He leered in his best imitation of a Drury Lane villain, then laughed when she pokered up in response. "Suspicious soul. I intend nothing more dangerous than to place your precious self in the hands of my housekeeper. She will show you to a room and make the garment as new. Come along now."

Ruth went.

Eleven

Paulo watched Secundus struggle with his cravat. "I thought today we were to go to London."

"We will if I can arrange it. May have to postpone it. Blast and bedamned." Sec added after another failed attempt with the cravat. "I'm told that upstart, Brummel, invented this devilish thing. I could wish the Regent had never taken him up!"

Paulo waited until the tie was tied. "So why do we not go to London?"

"Have to make arrangements so Ruth may go along for a few furbelows. Watched her with Rotherford yesterday. I've a notion there might be a match there. And if he's thinking of her now, when she's only the one decent dress to her name, seeing her in fashionable clothes ought to turn the trick."

"Miss Ruth wishes for this connection?"

"She's not confided in me, Paulo, but I've eyes in my head. I'll ask my Helen what she thinks, too, but first I've got to arrange for Ruth to leave the little ones. Helen's Miss Brown can care for them. Miss Brown is due any time now."

"Miss Brown has arrived and has settled in the nursery floor."

"Do I hear a problem?"

"It appears little Marie is not quite happy with the arrangement."

"Hmm. Miss Brown will cope and perhaps more easily if we are not here. But perhaps we should go to Brighton instead. It's closer if there is a problem. No, think it better be London . . ."

"Brighton. Where is this Brighton?"

"It's a seaside town which has taken the Prince Regent's fancy to an astonishing degree. Someone is supposed to have said his palace looks as if St. Paul's dome littered and had pups." Secundus shook his head. "People dyin' all over from hunger and want and the Regent spends a fortune on a play palace!"

"It is the way of princes, is it not?"

"Perhaps it is in your part of the world, Paulo, but in this country it is a disgrace and a shame." Sec patted his new coat, looked around to see if he'd forgotten anything, and headed for the door. "Now to find that slug-a-bed Gubby. He'll very likely know someone still in London who'll take us in while the women decide on the fol-de-rols my niece requires."

Secundus invaded Augustus's bedroom without a by-your-leave. He found his friend in bed sitting against a pile of pillows while his valet worked on his fingernails. His long-suffering friend didn't blink at Sec's request. Instead, he said that his intention, when he left the Alcesters, was to go on to Brighton, but there was no reason Sec couldn't use his town house in London. There would be, he insisted, not the least difficulty. "In fact, it will do the servants good to have something to do. It'll keep them on their toes. Just ask my majordomo for tickets to the opera or a play if you want that sort of thing. Ask him anything."

Secundus grimaced. "Theater? Don't know if I'm interested, but I suppose the women would like the treat."

"You'll enjoy it more than going to one of the Regent's musicals where I'll be suffering." Sec raised a brow. "It isn't the music to which I object," confided Augustus with a sigh. "It's the heat. You can't imagine what it does to one's shirt collars. Poor Prinny can't seem to tolerate even a hint of coolness. He'll have fires even now in the middle of August."

"Heat I can take. You've no notion of heat until you've lived in the East! But sour music? Or a bad play? Ah well, one does what one must, of course." He nodded. "Now that's settled, I'd better see my Helen and talk her into coming with us. She didn't answer when I asked her before. Simply isn't right, my Ruth going around a place like London with no woman in attendance."

"B-b-but Sec," said Helen not half an hour later, "I'm expected in Sheffield at the end of the week." Her eyes took on the glow they got when discussing things which interested her. "Would you believe its population has nearly doubled just since the turn of the century? A mere fifteen years? And already this year the price of bread, barley, and corn is near to doubling. There are hints of serious trouble there—the hunger, you know. I'm to give a lecture and, incidentally, inspect one of my charities where I've not been seen for far too long."

"A lecture? You can't postpone it?" Helen's mouth firmed, and her eyes grew very slightly cold. Sec looked chagrined. "No of course you can't. But what is to be done?"

"I don't suppose you could postpone taking Ruth to London? I wish to stay awhile in the north and study what might be done, but I could return immediately if you truly need me."

Secundus smiled widely. "I always thought you a wonderful lady, Helen. Now I know it. I'll tell you what. I'll just take Ruth sightseeing until you get there—except when I'm seeing to business. Got a letter from my factor and I'm needed, he says . . ." An arrested look crossed his features. "Helen, that makes no sense. I've been gone for fifteen years and never once been needed in London. Besides which, when I first arrived and met that man, I'd have sworn he was not happy to see me. But, I'm back less than a month and suddenly they can't do without me. Why is that, do you think?"

"It's perfectly obvious. How can he show you how important he is if you aren't around to be impressed?"

They shook their heads over the vagaries of human nature. "Well, however that may be, I want to do a bit of checking at the office and must see my solicitor about my will. Then I've another little errand to run." He said the last in an offhand way, but his eyes never left his love's face.

"So," she said, unaware he'd hinted at something of importance, "we're d-d-decided? I'm to give my lecture and you're to go to London and when I get back I'll take Ruth around to my modiste?"

Sec got red around the ears. He cleared his throat. "Eh, Helen, love . . ."

"Yes?"

"Hmmm. *Not* your modiste," he blurted.

For a moment Helen looked utterly blank. Then she glanced down at her plain and well-worn gown and chuckled. "I see what you mean, Sec. I'm certain Sir Augustus will know just whom you should patronize." She laughed again. "Don't look as if you feared I'd bite you. I make no pretense to fashion and you are correct that Ruth must not do the same."

"I'm glad you did not feel I'd insulted you. We can travel as far as London together, perhaps?"

Helen put on an exaggerated expression of shock. "Secundus, we can't!"

"Why not?"

"Ride miles with you in a closed carriage! My dear, I'd be ruined."

"No, no. Only compromised. I'd simply have to marry you out of hand." He dropped his teasing to remind her they'd not be alone; Ruth would be along. "So, are you truly against the notion, Helen?"

"I believe I'd enjoy it above anything! When do we leave?"

"Well, for myself, I could be ready in an hour, but I know it takes you ladies considerably longer."

"Yes." She nodded, widening her eyes. "All of two. I'm sorry to delay you by so many minutes," she added, tongue in cheek. "One very nice thing about being such an unfashionable creature, is that it doesn't take forever to do up my trunks and boxes. I'd not thought we could go so soon. Perhaps I may introduce Ruth to the modiste before leaving for the north and they may start the fittings, which will have us home all the sooner. Yes, that's an excellent notion." She lifted the large watch pinned to her dress and squinted at it. "About eleven then? It should take Ruth no longer than it does me, since she has no more wardrobe than I! Cook will put us up a basket so we need not stop. We should be in London by five, I think."

When Secundus returned home it was to find guests. He asked Paulo to see about packing, before entering the parlor, where he and an excited-looking Ruth exchanged glances. "Miss Chalmers, I believe," he said, bowing. "Mr. Chalmers. How do ye do?"

"Very well, thank you, Mr. Alcester," said Lucy's father so morosely that Sec had trouble keeping his countenance.

If Ruth looked excited, Miss Chalmers simply glowed.

Secundus turned to Ruth and raised a brow questioningly, but got nothing but a dimpled smile in answer. A horse was heard trotting up the lane and Miss Chalmers, blushing, excused herself.

Upon entering the hall from the bright sunshine, Robert's eyes adjusted slowly to the dimmer light. "Lucy." He shook his head, blinking, not believing he'd truly seen her. She touched his arm and, rising on tiptoe, also touched his cheek with her lips. "Lucy?" he asked, shocked.

"Yes, Robert. Aren't you pleased, m'love."

He held himself stiffly. "Should you be here?"

She smiled. "You'll find my father in the drawing room. I thought I should warn you and have watched for you."

Rob's tension grew. "You and your father have reached an agreement?"

"He and I have been talking practically ever since he came home from Rotherford's party yesterday."

"And?"

"Oh, Robert, he isn't happy about it, and still feels he's doing badly by me, but he's agreed."

"He'll allow me to pay my addresses?"

"You want it spelled out, do you not?" She smiled mistily. "I am to be allowed my choice of husband."

Robert's breath was released with a whoosh. "My love." He folded her gently into his arms and held her close.

When they strolled into the parlor a few minutes later, Mr. Chalmers surreptitiously wiped a tear from the corner of one eye. He squeezed Ruth's hand. "You were right," he said in a gruff voice. "She's happy and that is important."

Secundus explained that he was to take Ruth off to London and that Miss Rotherford was to return from her trip north to help Ruth order a new wardrobe.

Lucy clapped her hands. "Sir! I can't wait to see Ruth. She's magnificent even in her old and worn gowns. Just think what she'll be when properly dressed."

"I *have* thought," said Secundus with a wink.

When the Chalmerses left, Secundus went to Augustus's room and found him just ready to leave it. "London? Why London?" asked the aggrieved baronet. "Why must you run off so quickly when I've just arrived?"

"Oh, this and that." Secundus flipped his hand back and forth. "Mostly Ruth's wardrobe, but I had a confusing letter from my London factor. Can't make head nor tail of it. Then I've another errand or two. Anyway, can't dawdle. Helen's been expecting us anytime this last half hour. Did you, by chance, write that letter of introduction to your majordomo?"

"You make my head spin," complained Augustus. "But then," he said with a sigh, "you always did, did you not? Of course I've written the letter! Now I'll just have my traps packed and be off myself. No sense staying if you are away."

"You are welcome as long as you please, you know. Now I must be off."

Secundus took the stairs two at a time, hurrying down to where Paulo sat in the driver's seat of the landau. Luggage was strapped to the back, and Ruth, her head still spinning with the speed of it all, sat with her back to the horses. "Well, my dear?"

"I don't know if I'm on my heels or my head, Uncle Sec. You surely do things in a hurry. I'm totally bemused." A very small frown creased her brow. "I'm also worried about Marie. She isn't herself."

"She'll do just fine with Miss Brown," soothed Sec, "and you said yourself your brother is better at dealing with Marie than you are."

"I know it and I'll try not to worry." Ruth bit her lip.

* * *

Two days later Secundus stood beside Helen in the foyer of Augustus's town house and smiled down at her. "Well, my love?"

"Did I once wonder about *you* keeping up with *me?*"

Sec's brows rose. "I've a faint recollection of something like that."

"I erred, did I not? I wonder now, if *I* can keep up with *you!*"

"Of course you can, and if you cannot, then you must tell me and I will wait for you to catch up."

"I don't know if that is fair to you."

"Helen, don't you know I've run so fast only so I might *catch up to you?* Now I'll need to unlearn the trick of it. The carriage waits, love," he added, a sad look in his eye. "And the sooner you go, the sooner you may return."

Helen pursed her lips and held up one hand. She used the other to count off what had been done. "I took Ruth to the modiste where we choose several patterns for gowns. We went to the drapers where we chose materials and trim. Then we discussed hats at Madam Joie's. You say you'll see to having shoes made for the girl, and that leaves only unmentionables and silly accessories, such as parasols. You have the schedule of her fittings?"

"I do. If I cannot take her myself I will delegate the task to Paulo who will watch over her as carefully as you or I might do—or perhaps better. Both the Portuguese and the Goan cultures take great care of their young ladies, you know, and he was raised in a mixture of both." Helen looked around as if she were searching for something. "What is it, my dear?"

"I don't know?" She raised a bewildered-looking countenance and met his thoughtful gaze. "Sec, I have never felt so indecisive in my life. I'm sure of it."

"You are sure you feel indecisive?"

She chuckled, and when he held open his arms, she walked into them, ignoring the footman who stood near the stairs. "I'm a widgeon."

"That you are not. . . . Perhaps we've the same fear each time we part?"

She looked up at him. "That something will happen and we will be separated for good and all? You fear that, too?"

"I do."

"Will it ever go away?"

"I'm sure it will. Trust me?"

Helen tipped her head and blinked her eyes at him. "Sec?"

"Hmmm?"

"You'd better let me go now."

"I don't want to."

"But I must go."

"Hmmm."

The footman turned his back and raised his eyes to the ceiling. It was several long moments before he felt free to return to his accustomed position at the foot of the stairs.

"We go to see a bishop?" asked Paulo politely a day or so later, as their hackney crossed the Thames on the way to the archbishop's London palace. "In your Church of England, is that a special kind of priest?"

"Hm."

"Why do you need a priest, oh second son of Alcester?"

"Hm? Oh." Red tinged Sec's cheeks. "Never you mind."

"Perhaps I should not be here? I will be an e-cum-branch?"

"That's *encumbrance*, Paulo, and where do you get such

silly notions? You can't have wished to stay in that musty office, the clerks leaning over their ledgers, and that oily shark of a factor breathing down your neck."

"I, too, wonder about yon oily factor." Paulo rolled the adjective off his tongue, very nearly giving the insult an innocuous sound.

"I'll wonder another day. Once I've got my family sorted out."

"Is it for your family, then, that you have dressed in your very best new clothes as if for your own funeral and are sour and nervous and uncertain?"

"Sour and nervous, am I?" growled Sec. "Well, so you'd be, if your interests hung on the words of the man we're about to see."

"How does this unknown man control your interests, blessed second son?"

Secundus sighed. "I wish to buy a license from the man."

"A license to do what?" Paulo was nothing if not persistent in the pursuit of knowledge.

"In church last Sunday, the banns were being read. Remember?"

"It is necessary they be read three times if the young couple are to wed. Eldest son of the eldest son of Alcester explained it to me."

"Yes, and anyone wishing to marry must go through that, having one's business known by every here-and-therian in the parish. Well, I won't have it."

"And what will you have?" Paulo asked as the carriage drew to a halt.

"I'll have me a license, that's what I'll have. Then the vicar may marry one without banns. Perhaps I'll have a special license. With that one can be married anywhere. One need not even be in a church."

"Will this license be expensive?"

"I believe they don't come cheap. Come along." Sec turned back to the hackney driver who was loudly demanding his money. "You'll get your fare when I'm done with you. We'd never get another hackney if you go running off, and if I don't pay you, you won't. Run off, I mean. Your fare plus a *pourboire* will be a bagatelle after what I'll cough up here!"

Half an hour later they were done. "I'm glad one doesn't have to do *that* every day."

"Do we return to your office now?" Paulo asked. When Sec nodded, he added, "I would consider it a favor to be allowed to check that man's books."

"Would you, now?" asked Sec, surprised. "I wouldn't ask it of you—or anyone, Paulo—but if you're offering, I'll let you have at them."

"It is one of those things on which we don't agree, Sec. I find such problems fascinating. What yon oily factor has gotten up to is a puzzle for which I'll discover a solution."

The factor, when told Paulo was to be given access to the records, blustered about thievery on the docks and damage during long sea journeys, and was soon making excuses for problems of which Sec and Paulo were, as of yet, unaware, or, at best, had only vague suspicions.

"Well," said Secundus somewhat later, "I'm glad to see the last of him. He actually seemed to fear you, Paulo."

"It is my reputation, honored sir. It has come all this way across the seas before me. Soon your English employees will know I do nothing evil—only that I allow no evil from those serving you." Paulo bit his lip at that slip of the tongue, glancing at Sec as he did so. He relaxed when Sec laughed. Paulo leaned against the desk and waited for his old friend to undouble himself and wipe away the tears. "I do not often give you reason for such merriment," he said in a dry tone.

"So *that's* it. You've been angling to take over my

London office as your uncle has authority over the Bombay office," accused Sec. "I wonder how I could have been so doltish as to wonder why you wished to travel with me to England. Did you lose when your family drew lots to decide who should be sacrificed—coming all this way from hearth and home?"

"I wished to come. I was the obvious choice as well since I have a made a study of the English have I not?"

"And a study of me, I think." Sec grinned. "If it's what you want, Paulo, so be it." Sec looked at Paulo curiously. "You have had this in mind for a long time, have you not?"

"My uncle has had suspicions of the oily factor for some time."

"Never thought to tell me, I suppose?" grumbled Sec.

"You told him never to bother you with trivialities."

"Losses of the magnitude hinted at today can hardly be called trivial."

"It is worse than expected, true, but we planned to remedy all. It was not necessary for honorable Alcester to concern himself."

"In your own good time. Just when, Paulo, were *we* planning to leave for England?"

Paulo grinned. "Soon."

"If that letter hadn't caught up with me, would we still be in India?"

Paulo shrugged. "Perhaps."

"Paulo, in England we say tomorrow, or next week. *Not* next month, next year."

Paulo smiled. "I am in England now. I will do as the English do. You will go, now, and settle your family. You will marry your lady, and, after a time, you will be interested in business. Then when we may see each other often, we may discuss my methods."

"I suppose I had better get back." He looked up startled. "Paulo, we'll be done soon and going back to the country. You can't stay in London! You must attend my wedding before settling in here."

Paulo smiled. "But you cannot do all at once, can you? It will be necessary to discuss settlements with young Robert's lady's father. That one will not be satisfied easily! And I believe I heard rumors of parties and such like. So, I will stay here where I am needed. When you have decided on a wedding date, it will be an honor and a joy to attend the solemn rites for the second son of most honored Alcester." Paulo bowed.

"Not rites, Paulo. That sounds too much like a burial! We will have a marriage service."

"Rites, service, ceremony . . ." Paulo shrugged. "It will, in any case, bring me great joy to see you attain your happiness."

Red behind the ears, Sec had nothing more to say.

Twelve

Unexpectedly, Rotherford appeared in London. Ruth was alone in the drawing room reading a book when he was announced. He immediately suggested he leave.

"Because I'm unchaperoned?" she asked. He nodded. "I will ring for the housekeeper then. There is enough of her to satisfy the highest of sticklers."

A comfortably fat and motherly presence was soon seated with her sewing at the far end of the room. "What has brought you to London, my lord?" asked Ruth.

He very nearly responded, "You, my dear." Finally, he said he had business with his solicitor—which he had, but normally that gentleman would have driven down to Rotherford. "How are you?" he asked.

"In a dream. I never thought to visit such a house as this or to order such wonderful gowns as my uncle insists I have. He is exceedingly generous."

"I wish my sister would order a few things."

"She did order one gown, a soft blue silk with a narrow border of lace at the neck and the bottom of the sleeves." Ruth shook her head, wryly. "Then she felt guilty for what she called frivolity. Oh! Uncle Secundus, you're home early, are you not?"

"I finished my business. Now, with Helen arriving today, we may have a few days for sightseeing and what-not while your order is completed. Good day, Rotherford. Did I hear," Sec continued without waiting for a response from their guest, "that my Helen ordered a new gown from your modiste?" Ruth nodded. "Good, good." A devilish glint appeared in his eye.

"What are you planning, Uncle Sec."

"Planning? Me?" He rubbed his nose. "Why, nothing at all. What brings you to town, Rotherford? Now, that was an impertinent question, was it not?" he asked, flicking an amused glance toward Ruth. "Where are you staying? A hotel? Nonsense. You must come to us."

Later that evening, Alcester and Rotherford stopped outside Ruth's room. From inside came feminine laughter. "Helen sounds happy, doesn't she?" asked Sec. "I feared, when she agreed to return from the north more quickly than she wished, that she'd be troubled."

"There's never been but one man who could make her do what she didn't wish to do. For you, she'd stand on her head in the Queen's drawing room."

"And you don't understand it."

"No." Rotherford sighed. "I admit I don't understand it."

"Hmm. I wonder if you'd stand on yours if my niece asked it of you."

Every inch of John's exposed skin reddened. "Am I so obvious?"

"A man in love recognizes that state in another," said Sec, kindly.

"Love."

Sec stared. "Surely you aren't still denying you know what it is!"

"Do I? I know I get cold all over when I think she may turn down my suit. And for the first time in my life I've experienced true jealousy. They say one can't feel that if there is no love, but . . ."

"Believe me," said Sec, dryly, "you know." Just then they again heard Helen's contralto laugh and its counterpart—Ruth's lighter chuckle. "Sounds like they'll be awhile, does it not? Shall we?" Sec gestured toward the stairs.

Rotherford followed Alcester into the library. "I've taken a box for the opera, hoping you might be free some evening," he said. "Covent Garden will be full of mushrooms at this time of year, but it is, I'm told, a reasonably good production. I thought Miss Alcester might enjoy it."

"We must ask her, of course," Sec said. "It was a kind thought."

Rotherford flushed slightly and admitted, "Shall I be honest? I could think of no other acceptable way of spending the evening so near to her."

Sec chuckled. "I'll use it as an excuse for sitting beside my Helen and, when no one is looking, holding her hand."

Both men were laughing when the women walked in. It was the motif for the days which followed—laughter. Helen wondered at it; John was amazed by it; Ruth revelled in it. And Secundus? Secundus never gave it a thought. How else should life be, after all, when one was involved in nothing of a serious nature? He saw his Helen's growing happiness and felt as if all were right with his world.

It was too special, too perfect. It couldn't last. Sec returned home one day and was handed a note from Helen. A very angry note indeed. He grimaced and wondered who had tipped the double to his love. He sighed, and, taking back his hat and cane, went out the door, crossed the busy road, and entered the park in the middle of the square where Helen paced a short section of path well screened from prying eyes.

The park was very nearly deserted at this hour, which was why Helen chose it for their confrontation. The Falconer house was, in the way of town houses, too small to achieve privacy for an argument and an argument, thought Sec, they would have. Helen's temper was obviously no sweeter for having waited nearly half a day. She was furious.

"How dare h . . !" he heard her mutter.

Sec watched his love before approaching her, a rueful look about his eyes. He wondered how she'd discovered his latest ruse. From the tenor of her note it was obvious she had. Ah well. Very likely the modiste had done the deed. Poor Helen. She hadn't a notion of how he wished to pamper her, to give her the whole world and the moon as well!

But she must discover he wasn't to be ruled, which he guessed might be her present goal. She was nicely angry, wasn't she?

"Well, Helen?"

"There you are!"

"As you asked me to be, m'dear."

"Don't you 'dear' m-m-me, you . . . you . . ."

"Philanderer?" Secundus kept his features bland with great difficulty.

"What? No, of course not. Why should I think a thing like that?" she asked suspiciously.

"I don't know." Laughter bubbled up, but, aware it would be unappreciated, Sec controlled it. "Philandering just seems a thing women have on their minds when they're angry at their men."

"That's nonsense. I think." Helen blinked, then eyed Secundus narrowly for a long moment. She tipped her head. "You didn't m-m-mention such a thing because you've a guilty conscience, did you?"

"No such thing," he said, chuckling. "Have you calmed

enough we may discuss whatever it is which has you so hot and bothered?"

Helen's teeth clashed together. Twice.

"I see you have not. Let me think up another means by which I may divert you. I'll not fight with you, m'love," he added when she rounded on him. "When you are ready to talk about . . . whatever . . . then I'll be as sober as a bishop. Until then I'll do my best to make you laugh."

"But that's not fair, Sec." Helen actually pouted.

"In what way is it unfair?"

"I get over my vexation much more quickly when I may rant and rave and then *do* something."

"Hmmm. I see." Sec rubbed his nose. "We've a problem."

"We do?"

"Afraid so. You see when I rant and rave I am doing something. For instance I'm firing some incompetent soul who has been given every chance and who has finally made such a fine botch of things that I've lost patience. I don't believe I'll ever feel like ranting at *you*, my dear," he added softly.

Helen strolled beside him, her lip between her teeth as she considered. "Sec, do you think you might let me rant just a little?"

"Well now." He gave her a teasing look. "Perhaps . . . five minutes?"

"Oh, f-f-five minutes would be quite sufficient—for most of my tantrums, at least." She added, "I can say a very great deal in five minutes."

"Then we'll agree that, with proper notice, you'll have five minutes for ranting whenever you are in a temper. After that I'll divert you in any way I think appropriate. Is that an acceptable compromise?"

She chuckled. "I reserve the right to adjust the five-minute limit if I find, too often, it is insufficient. Now, I've a fine rant saved up for you, and though you've taken the edge off it, it is still there rankling away."

"Shall we be comfortable, then? There's a bench surrounded by bushes making it as private as can be. I, at least, prefer to be seated. I'll not be bothered if you choose to pace or to tower over me, and if anyone observes my ungentlemanly behavior—well, at this hour, no one is likely to, are they?" They sat at extreme ends of the bench. Sec, watch in hand, waited. She turned to him. "Ready, my love?" he asked.

"Quite ready." She drew in a deep breath and he opened the watch. "Now, I have been given to understand, Secundus Alcester, that you have done an unforgivable thing. You should not have done it," she went on before he could insert he hoped she didn't actually mean *unforgivable*. "You may not buy me gowns. It is not done." She bit her lip, throwing him a sideways glance. "Perhaps you were away so long you forgot?"

"Sorry. Can't use that as an excuse. Know it isn't proper."

Helen frowned. "Then I cannot understand it. How dare you tell that modiste to make up half a dozen gowns for me?"

"Your five minutes aren't up, Helen."

"Oh. I forgot. I will not have it, Sec. I do not spend a great deal on myself, as I once told you. You actually ordered a lace gown suitable for a royal drawing room! Of what possible use is that to a woman such as myself? Lace! An outrageous expense! *Never* do such a thing again."

"I'm not allowed to buy you gifts, Helen?" he asked in a meek voice.

"Money should not be wasted on frivolity." Her face set into firm lines, and her arms crossed over her chest.

"It is my money," he said, still meek-seeming.

"But I don't wish for such silly things, Sec."

"But if I wish to give them to you?"

"Well," she said sternly, quite as if it were settled, "you can't. Most especially, you can't give an unmarried woman personal gifts unless you wish to ruin her."

"But I haven't given them to you."

Helen blinked. Thoughts of the demi-mondaine entered her head. She turned horrified eyes his way. "Sec, did I err? Was t-t-that order not for me but for a ladybi— I mean, were those gowns for me or were they not?"

"I wonder if I should answer that. I think I'll be damned if they are and damned if they aren't! But, yes, they are for you."

"Then . . ." She looked totally bewildered.

"Your five minutes are up, love."

"Oh bother five minuteses."

He chuckled and moved a trifle closer. "Helen, I would never deliberately compromise you." She turned her nose up and away. "I'd like to know who let the cat out of the bag. You were not supposed to know of them until it was proper."

"You mean a wedding gift?" Her eyes widened. "Oh, Sec."

He distracted her quite nicely by kissing her. Thoroughly.

"I thought you would do nothing which would compromise me," she said, snuggling closer.

He ostentatiously looked around. "I don't believe there's a soul in sight. Therefore you can't possibly be compromised. Shall we return to the house? After one more kiss just to keep me in practice?"

"No more kisses," she said a trifle breathlessly. "I think you've quite enough practice as it is. But you needn't think we've settled this problem of you spending money on me when it isn't something I need."

"But of course we have. I've no intention of giving anything so improper as clothing to an unmarried woman."

"But even when I'm a married woman . . ."

"Then you will have promised to obey your husband, will you not?"

Helen bit her lip. "Sec," she said in a rather small voice, looking up at him with a worried expression, "Sec, I don't know if I can promise that!"

He laughed. "Oh, my love, my dearest love. We'll make a private agreement that when that part of the marriage service is read, it will be understood between us that you mean you'll promise to *try*. Will that do?"

"Maybe," she said, still uncertain. "But," she added sternly, "I do not approve of lace."

Sec rubbed his nose. "I rather hoped you'd take Ruth to Court. She's never been presented, you know."

Helen's eyes widened. "I hadn't thought of that. Surely someone must." Helen stood up and stared at him thoughtfully. "You have the right of it—about the lace, I mean, which is required by etiquette. I suppose it will make you insufferable." He laughed but didn't deny it. She grinned. "I never noticed ranting was work, but I am ever so ready to eat. Shall we go?"

They strolled slowly back across the street, fairly satisfied with their compromise—at least, the compromise each believed they'd reached.

And, although she'd not admit it, Helen looked forward to the new gowns. It was against her principles to spend money on herself when so many needed so much, but the notion of several new gowns in the latest style and the nicest of fabrics was appealing. Besides, she couldn't insult her love by refusing his gifts—when he finally gave them to her—could she?

Which would be *when?* After all, the silly man had yet to propose. Simply assuming they'd get married—which they seemed to have done—wasn't proper. Helen slid a sideways glance at her Sec. Surely he *would* propose. Surely he didn't think that, at some point, they'd just set a date and get married. Or did he?

Oh dear. Was she going to be so ridiculously missish she'd regret Sec hadn't offered in proper form? Her lip between her teeth, Helen lectured herself sternly. She had what she'd given up believing might ever be: she had her Secundus returned to her.

But, despite that joy—and it was great joy—Helen's heart was sore at the thought of the children Sec didn't want, the children she'd never have—children, if she were honest, she'd never thought to have. What of the orphans whom, over the years, she'd given a chance at a decent life? Weren't they hers? In a way? And the young Alcesters, too. And, eventually, her brother's children. How silly of me, she thought. I've children of the heart and children related to me. I must not wish for the moon but be thankful for what I have.

And I *will* be, she told herself, after regretting, for a moment, the never-to-be children of her body—and regretting, just a little, that she'd not have that very special memory of Secundus romantically asking for her hand.

Thirteen

Three days after her return home, the morning dawned gloriously fine, so Ruth put on one of her old gowns and went outside. She was determined to finish the flower bed around the still empty fountain and was perhaps a quarter of the way around it when she was interrupted.

"Lord Rotherford! You startled me." Ruth lay aside her trowel.

He held a hand to her to help her up. "How many times must I remind you you've agreed you'd call me John?" he said plaintively.

Ruth was a trifle miffed that she had seen nothing of the man since their return from London several days earlier. And after raising her hopes that he was actually interested in courting her, too. "*You* agreed. I don't think I've agreed to anything at all."

"Hmmm. That sounded just the teeniest bit pettish. I believe you need a refreshing drive. The moving air will cool your temper."

"It will, will it?" A wary expression took up residence on John's face. Ruth lifted her nose a trifle higher. "You're certain?" she goaded when he said no more.

"Far less certain than a moment ago. How have I offended?"

"I think by assuming you knew better than I what

would do me good." His eyes narrowed. Ruth, never one to hold a grudge, was feeling better the longer they talked. "The fact you are correct is," she said, with a toss to her head, "quite irrelevant." Back to teasing with him, she could smile.

John relaxed when he saw her dimple come and go. "Now, that I didn't know. If I'm in the right, how could that put me in the wrong?"

"It's one of those perversities which make women female."

His eyebrow quirked. "If *I'd* said that I'd be very much in the wrong, would I not?"

"Of course," she agreed, wide-eyed. "It is a category of perverse things. For instance, little Tibby may criticize Peter all she wishes, but let anyone else try it and she jumps right in to defend him."

"*Will* you come for a drive? Please?"

"I must change."

"You look delightful just as you are." He held out his hand. "Come?"

"Delightful?" She gave him a wry look. He laughed, but still held out his hand. She took it. Nearly a mile passed, nicely filled with conversation concerning their London jaunt when Ruth straightened in her seat. "Why have we turned here? Where are we going?"

"I thought we'd go to Rother Hall." Ruth made an aborted motion toward her dress. She settled back and sighed. "You think I should have allowed you time to make a grand toilet before appearing before my toffy-nosed butler? Don't trouble yourself, my dear. Maden has closed his eyes to Helen's odd style of dressing for years; he will feel nothing but relief at your appearance, m'love, despite that interesting touch of green about the knees."

Ruth ignored that bit of provocation. "Is Helen still there?" she asked quietly.

"I wouldn't take you to my home were there not a suitable chaperon," he said in a reproving tone.

"Don't lecture," she pleaded. Assured the proprieties were satisfied, she reversed herself and said, "Besides, even if she weren't there, surely I'm too old for the gossips to worry about such things."

"Neither too old nor too unattractive. You are, in fact, a delight."

"I've done it again, have I not?"

"What?" he asked.

She dipped her head, softly admitting, "Made it necessary for you to hand out absurd compliments."

"I wonder where you came by this odd notion that you don't deserve them." He noted how her lips drooped slightly at the corners and searched for a means of cheering her. "When Gerry first saw you," he told her, "he came home and asked me who the local goddess might be. Does that sound as if you are unattractive?"

"Goddess!" Ruth blushed rosily, the heat drawing her hands up to hide her embarrassment. "Oh, dear. Yes, actually it does. I can't imagine wishing to be friendly with a goddess. How very uncomfortable it would be."

John shouted with laughter, startling his team. He brought them back under control. "My dear delight, why ever did it take so long to find you?"

"I don't know. Tell me."

He turned a grin her way. "You're learning, are you not? That was definitely a flirtatious request."

"I thought I'd done it rather well," she said complacently, but added quickly, "however, I don't think I could manage much more of a like nature just now."

He chuckled, but obliged her by accepting the hint they change the subject. "Tell me how Brownie is getting along with the young ones. I understand she discovered those girls at my party told Marie governesses were nasty and mean. Has she soothed the child's fears?"

"She has." Then Ruth described Tibby's grumbles concerning the necessity of doing much hated embroidery— a plot to help Marie gain confidence. Tibby had explained to Ruth, just as Miss Brown explained it to Tibby, how Marie could do very nice embroidery and, finding she could do something better than her big sister would, confided Tibby, surprise Marie very much. "Tibby hates to embroider."

"But, for her sister's sake, she will do it?"

"Yes. Tibby is nothing if not thorough. She'll do no grumbling when Marie is around. You will laugh when you see the result of her labor."

"I predict it will be quite the ugliest sampler since Helen's. And what else has been happening with the Alcesters?" She told him of Mr. Chalmers's reluctant change of heart. With the settlements approved, the engagement was now official. By then they'd arrived. He reached up to help her from the rather high curricle seat, grasping her waist and lifting her down.

Ruth put her hands on his shoulders and felt that odd tingling surge through her. "John?" She gazed at him, froze, almost fearful, more than a little excited . . . wondered what he was thinking. She blinked rapidly.

"That bemused look, my love, is just the hint I've looked for since coming to you today. Marry me?" Ruth lips parted and her breath came rather quickly. "Soon?"

"John . . ."

"Ah, I was forgetting, was I not?" His hands tightened momentarily on her waist before he released her. He pulled at his trouser leg and then knelt on one knee, one hand going to cover his heart. "Miss Alcester, will you do me the honor of accepting my humble request of your hand in holy wedlock?" She blushed. "My fortune is yours. I place my heart beneath your dainty feet. Treat it carefully. Please? Don't trample it into the dust"—he glanced down—"er, gravel?"

"John, get up off the ground at once. I refuse to marry a fool."

"I've never been thought a fool and I don't now consider myself so," he said, not moving from his position at her feet. He tipped his head to the side and gave her a solemn look. "Ruth?"

"Will you get up?" she hissed.

John ignored the fact they were not alone. "Not until you say yes."

Ruth glanced at an under gardener, the head gardener, and a grinning stable boy who held the heads of the restless team. At the last she looked at Maden, who stared at the two of them with such an indulgent expression it brought a deeper flush to her cheeks. "Oh, dear."

"You see," he confided, "if I stay here with my staff looking on, you are too kind to tell me no. They might laugh at me if you do, mightn't they?" He spoke lightly, but his eyes were saying other, much more serious things. "Ruth?"

"Oh very well." Giving in to his wishes which were, indeed, her own, she got into the spirit of his very public proposal. "You do me great honor, my lord. I accept heart and fortune and promise to treat both with care."

His lordship let out a whoop more appropriate to Peter. He rose to his feet and drew her to him. He wasn't entirely lost to good sense, however, and merely whispered in her ear that she must wait for greater privacy before he allowed himself their first kiss.

"John," called Helen, "stop embarrassing that poor girl and bring her here where I, too, may give her a hug. Ruth, are you truly fool enough to take on my dear tyrant of a brother? He will bully you and cajole you and try to tell you how to go on."

"Dear Helen," interjected the dear tyrant politely, "do you think you might wait until after our vows are taken before denigrating my personality too thoroughly? You might frighten Ruth off. I don't think I could bear it."

Tears brightened Helen's eyes. "John?"

"If you felt for another Alcester half what I feel for Ruth, then I must apologize for that particular bit of interference in your life."

Helen came to him and hugged him. "If he hadn't come home to me, I might hate you for it, John. But Sec *has* come and, since neither of us has wasted the years, I won't repine." She searched his eyes. "I'm glad you've learned to love, John."

"Am I hearing correctly? Are you marrying my uncle?" asked Ruth.

"We're certainly thinking of it. Do you mind?"

"Not at all. In fact I think it a wonderful idea. Except— Oh, dear!" Ruth's dimples quivered, leapt into existence. "I've just had a thought. If you marry my uncle and I marry your brother, have you any notion just exactly what relationship we'll have to each other?"

Helen stared at Ruth. Reprehensibly Ruth giggled. Helen covered her mouth with her hand. "Oh, dear," she said when she could speak. "How very complicated it will be. How will we explain it?"

"Why bother? On alternate days, you may play first at being Ruth's aunt and then at being her sister." Rotherford nodded in a satisfied way. "That should confuse everyone quite nicely."

Epilogue

Shortly after returning from London, Secundus had an urgent message from Paulo which sent him straight back. Now they'd returned together, and after a bit of careful organization, Sec had come to see his love. He stopped in the path between the hedges and mopped his brow. Helen awaited him today by the summer house. It had been a very busy morning, and a wasted one if this next business didn't come right. He took one more swipe at his forehead before moving to stand under the trellis arch. "Well, Helen?"

"Is it well, Sec?" She peered across the mossy flagstones to where her love was framed by the climbing roses. "Come tell me, m'dear."

He seated himself on the stone bench and, for a moment, simply enjoyed the warmth of the sun and the sweet smell of the roses. "Well, now." He lifted one of Helen's hands and played with the fingers. "I think I have it sorted out."

"The trusts for the youngsters?"

"Hmm. Peter's reverts to him when he's twenty-five. The little girls will have excellent dowries or, if they don't marry, the income. I've fixed Marie's so her capital will always be in a trust fund." He smiled down at Helen and she tipped her head, a question in her eyes. "Wait, m'love. We'll get to us in a moment. First, my family. Agreed?"

"Tell me about Ruth and Robert, then."

"Ruth will have control of her monies immediately. It is hers absolute just as you wished. She is a sensible girl and won't play ducks and drakes with it if I'm a judge." He glanced at her. "Nor can it fall into the hands of a husband."

"Good. Because she and John became engaged while you were gone."

"Engaged? Well, now." He rubbed his nose. "I rather thought they might, but not quite so quickly. The settlements for Miss Chalmers are agreed to, so that leaves Robert."

Helen smiled and squeezed his hand. "I hope you've done well by him. Mr. Chalmers has allowed Lucy her choice, and the settlements have helped, but he still isn't happy. So. What have you done?"

"First, I set aside shares in my business."

"That will give them income during the coming bad times, when the farms . . . but now is no time for repining about the economy. Tell me what else you've done, please?"

"Well, I settled monies on Robert, too, of course. He'll need funds on which he may immediately draw. We fixed up things around the manor, but he wishes to adopt modern farming methods. His wife will wish to make changes inside the manor which is, as you know, pretty shabby. It all costs, Helen." He searched his mind and nodded. "That takes care of the lot of them, I think."

"Rob will do well by the 1-1-land, Sec." She raised their clasped hands to play with his fingers. "It's odd, isn't it? Usually, in a f-f-family, there is one interest which is p-p-passed on from generation to generation. In yours it should be seafaring."

"Well, there's Peter."

"Yes. P-P-Peter will do well at s-s-sea, I think." She looked at him. "But you. You went East and came back a n-n-nabob. B-b-business obviously suits you, doesn't it? And Robert. He has f-f-farming in his blood, I think. The girls are each d-d-different, one from the other."

"Helen, you are stammering far more than usual. Are you talking about the children to avoid talking about us?"

She blushed prettily. "I t-t-think maybe I am."

"I love you, you know."

"I know. I l-l-love you, t-t-too." She swallowed and said firmly, "Is it enough, Sec?"

"I think so. I hope so. It is all I have to give you since you've no greedy interest in my fortune." He grasped both her hands tightly, staring down at her bent head.

"But I'm so old," she said so softly he had to bend his own head to hear her. "We never did settle it—not really—about getting you an heir and, Sec, I cannot believe you don't wish one."

"Helen, I've waited forever, just to see you again. I never thought to do more than see you. Now, finding you free—well, it is more than I ever believed possible. There are ways to prevent children, you know." His hands gripped hers until she winced; he immediately loosened his hold. "Don't you understand, Helen? You are all that's important in my world."

"No woman was ever given a more loving testimony. But l-l-later . . ."

He touched her lips, quieting her. "Allow me to know my own mind?"

For just a moment she froze, her poor eyes misty, regretting one last time the children she'd never have. Then, pursing her lips, she kissed his finger. "It is what I ask for myself, is it not? Then I must be g-g-generous and allow you the same privilege. Very well. I will cease to worry the point. But," she said firmly, "there are others."

"You mean your many charities? Of course, you must continue as you will. For my peace of mind, I'd prefer to know exactly where you go and, when I feel it is dangerous, I reserve the right to argue the necessity." He shrugged. "When one loves, one worries, but no one can protect another completely—not when duty is involved. But you will discuss such things with me? Where we find ways of doing what you wish without danger, will you change your ways?"

Again Helen was silent for a long moment. "You, too? You will discuss with me what you must do?"

"Just you try to stop me. How can you think I'd not talk about my doings? Have you ever known me able to keep my own counsel? It will be part of our agreement, love, that you are required to listen to me boring on and on and on. You will become quite tired of it, I fear."

Helen laughed. "I doubt it. What I fear is that if there is trouble, at the docks, say, you'll be in the middle and then come tell me about it."

"Yes, there may be times when something must be done immediately. Will you take a man of my choice with you if you find yourself in such a position?" He lifted her face to look down into it. "He will be unobtrusive, my love, but he will guard you for me."

Helen remembered her fear the last time she'd gone among a group of angry men. She'd mastered it and learned what she needed to know, but she'd wondered if someone would carry out his threats to do her an injury. "I will reserve the right to approve of your choice, but we will find such a man."

"Now, have we spoken of everything?"

"Well, you once mentioned we might have Tibby and Marie to stay with us off and on." She got that mischievous look he loved. "That requires somewhere to keep a bed on which they may lay their heads at night."

"We, too, may wish a place to lay . . . our heads." She blushed at the innuendo he'd meant her to catch. "We'll use our wedding trip as an excuse to look for a good property not too far from here and not too far from London . . . near Tunbridge Wells, perhaps? Or—but, we can discuss where another time. What else, my love?"

"I can't t-t-think of a t-t-thing."

Sec, a trifle stiffly, got to his knees and took back her hands. "You know, Helen, I thought I'd feel awfully silly in this position."

"Do you not?" She smiled, her eyes warm and her heart beating faster. She *would* have memories. "You don't feel even a little strange?"

"Not a bit of it." His grip tightened slightly on her hands. "Helen, my one and only love, will you be mine?"

"It is the dearest wish of my heart."

"And mine." He got to his feet still holding her hands so that she, too, rose. He drew her gently into his embrace. "Right away, Helen?"

Her mouth drooped sadly and she shook her head. "With all the weddings which must be arranged, I fear it will be some time before we may organize our own. Well, it can't be helped," sighed Helen.

Sec kissed her, the kiss growing in warmth. When he held her slightly away from him and looked into her bemused face, he smiled. "Do you still think we should wait?"

"Sec, t-t-there is Ruth and John. Robert and Lucy. Should we take our h-h-happiness at the expense of theirs?"

"We've waited many years for happiness, Helen. I think they can wait a bit for theirs. Besides, why may we not be married at once and take our wedding trip later, once we've got them off on theirs?"

Helen chuckled. "I doubt John will allow Ruth time to buy a trousseau. He will take her to Paris, he says, and they'll choose it together. He's asked the vicar to post the banns. Lucy is to have a six months' engagement, I believe."

"Then we will get ourselves married right now. We'll travel between Ruth's marriage and Robert's, if that's all right with you."

"We can't get married right now."

"Can we not? I've no wish to let you go, so will you do me the favor of reaching inside my coat and there, in an inside pocket, you'll find a rather stiff document?" Rather shyly Helen dipped a hand under his coat. "Yes. That. You may read it, m'love." Holding the still-folded document under hands pressed against his chest, Helen flushed to the roots of her hair. She didn't know where to look. "You don't wish to read it?" he asked.

"Blast you Secundus Alcester!" She drew in a deep breath and let it out in a huff. "I'd hoped to keep it from you a trifle longer." She peered up at him. "I am," she said with dignity, "very nearly as blind as a bat. I can't read your precious paper without the aid of a glass."

"Why don't you wear spectacles?" he asked with masculine naïveté.

She debated telling him what she thought of that suggestion, but it didn't seem quite the right time. Instead she scowled to show her disapproval before laying her forehead against his chest. "Sec?" she asked a trifle shyly.

"Hm?"

"W-w-will you tell me what it is I'm holding in my hand?"

"Have you not guessed?"

"Do you suppose the vicar will be in about now?"

"Shall we go see?"

Helen giggled. "Are we eloping, Sec?"

He held her away from him and blinked. "Why, I believe we are."

"You see? I was right, wasn't I?"

"When you came to me fifteen years ago and said that we should elope?"

"Hm."

"I guess you must have been. It's just taken me a very long time to admit it." Sec took out his watch and looked at it. He smiled at Helen and crooked his arm. "Shall we go?"

Sec had planned carefully. Awaiting them in the vicar's parlor were their relatives and a few other people important to them. Paulo stood beside the vicar and Miss Brown softly played the piano. There were tears in Helen's eyes when Tibby gave her a bouquet of garden flowers done up with ribbons, more tears when her brother hugged her and told her to be happy. But, once they stood before the vicar, she felt nothing but a deep glow of happiness as she listened to Secundus making his vows.

She said her own with equal firmness and a sidelong look as she vowed to obey. When she saw Sec's tightly held lips and the twinkle in his eye, she very nearly succumbed to the giggles. Since it would have been very difficult to explain why they were laughing in the middle of one of life's most solemn moments, she manfully restrained herself.

Later the newly married couple stood near the French doors in the Rother Hall drawing room and looked around. Miss Brown had Tibby and Marie beside her and was earnestly answering some question Tibby had asked. Gerry, leaning on the back of their sofa, had an appreciative grin on his face as he unashamedly eavesdropped on the conversation between governess and child.

John and Ruth had their heads together and looked a trifle mazed from the strength of the feelings between them.

Across the room, Robert, Lucy's hand in his, talked with Mr. Chalmers, who beamed. Secundus had finally admitted in the man's presence to being a nabob. Mr. Chalmers was a happy man and already well on the way to believing he'd always approved his daughter's marriage, always known it would be a proper match.

Paulo stood quietly near the fireplace, a contented expression on his face as he met Sec's eyes across the room. Sir Augustus beamed.

Sec looked at Helen, who smiled back at him. With no need to consult, they strolled out into the shrubbery.

"Well, Helen?" asked Sec.

"It's very well, is it not?"

They stood beneath the rose-covered arch and he put his arms around her, drew her close. "I think all promises have been redeemed," he said thoughtfully.

"I think so, too, my love. Everything seems to have arranged itself very nicely."

He tipped his head and asked, "So now it is appropriate that we think only of ourselves?"

Their eyes met; the warmth of the look drew them still closer together.

"Do you agree, my Helen?" he whispered.

She did.

Silently, she praised her foresight in telling Maden to see the Lady's Garden was off-limits for the rest of the day. The vine-covered pavilion with its amply cushioned furniture had seen most of their stormy history. It seemed entirely proper it witness the scene which held the promise of a sunny future.

BOOK YOUR PLACE ON OUR WEBSITE AND MAKE THE READING CONNECTION!

We've created a customized website just for our very special readers, where you can get the inside scoop on everything that's going on with Zebra, Pinnacle and Kensington books.

When you come online, you'll have the exciting opportunity to:

- View covers of upcoming books
- Read sample chapters
- Learn about our future publishing schedule (listed by publication month *and author*)
- Find out when your favorite authors will be visiting a city near you
- Search for and order backlist books from our online catalog
- Check out author bios and background information
- Send e-mail to your favorite authors
- Meet the Kensington staff online
- Join us in weekly chats with authors, readers and other guests
- Get writing guidelines
- AND MUCH MORE!

**Visit our website at
http://www.kensingtonbooks.com**

More Regency Romance
From Zebra